A MERCY

Fiction

Love
Paradise
Jazz
Beloved
Tar Baby
Song of Solomon
Sula
The Bluest Eye

Non-Fiction

The Dancing Mind
Playing in the Dark:
Whiteness and the Literary Imagination

Wyandotts
L. Ontario
Neuter Nation
L. Erie
Erigas
Andastes
Potomuck
Miami R.
Kenhawa R.
Guyandott R.
James
Tuscaroras
Woccons
Catawbas
Cheraws

A Mercy

Toni Morrison

Chatto & Windus
LONDON

Published by Chatto & Windus 2008
Published in the United States of America in 2008 by Alfred A. Knopf

2 4 6 8 10 9 7 5 3 1

First published in Great Britain in 2008 by
Chatto & Windus
Random House, 20 Vauxhall Bridge Road,
London SW1V 2SA
www.rbooks.co.uk

Addresses for companies within The Random House Group Limited can be found at:
www.randomhouse.co.uk/offices.htm

The Random House Group Limited Reg. No. 954009

A CIP catalogue record for this book
is available from the British Library

Hardback ISBN 9780701180454
Trade Paperback ISBN 9780701183417

The Random House Group Limited supports The Forest Stewardship
Council (FSC), the leading international forest certification organisation. All our
titles that are printed on Greenpeace approved FSC certified paper carry the FSC logo.
Our paper procurement policy can be found at
www.rbooks.co.uk/environment

Mixed Sources
Product group from well-managed
forests and other controlled sources
www.fsc.org Cert no. TT-COC-2139
© 1996 Forest Stewardship Council
FSC

Printed and bound in Great Britain by
Clays Ltd, St Ives plc

Don't be afraid. My telling can't hurt you in spite of what I have done and I promise to lie quietly in the dark—weeping perhaps or occasionally seeing the blood once more—but I will never again unfold my limbs to rise up and bare teeth. I explain. You can think what I tell you a confession, if you like, but one full of curiosities familiar only in dreams and during those moments when a dog's profile plays in the steam of a kettle. Or when a corn-husk doll sitting on a shelf is soon splaying in the corner of a room and the wicked of how it got there is plain. Stranger things happen all the time everywhere. You know. I know you know. One question is who is responsible? Another is can you read? If a pea hen refuses to brood I read it quickly and, sure enough, that night I see a minha mãe standing hand in hand with her little boy, my shoes jamming the pocket of her apron.

Other signs need more time to understand. Often there are too many signs, or a bright omen clouds up too fast. I sort them and try to recall, yet I know I am missing much, like not reading the garden snake crawling up to the door saddle to die. Let me start with what I know for certain.

The beginning begins with the shoes. When a child I am never able to abide being barefoot and always beg for shoes, anybody's shoes, even on the hottest days. My mother, a minha mãe, is frowning, is angry at what she says are my prettify ways. Only bad women wear high heels. I am dangerous, she says, and wild but she relents and lets me wear the throwaway shoes from Senhora's house, pointy-toe, one raised heel broke, the other worn and a buckle on top. As a result, Lina says, my feet are useless, will always be too tender for life and never have the strong soles, tougher than leather, that life requires. Lina is correct. Florens, she says, it's 1690. Who else these days has the hands of a slave and the feet of a Portuguese lady? So when I set out to find you, she and Mistress give me Sir's boots that fit a man not a girl. They stuff them with hay and oily corn husks and tell me to hide the letter inside my stocking—no matter the itch of the sealing wax. I am lettered but I do not read what Mistress writes and Lina and Sorrow cannot. But I know what it means to say to any who stop me.

My head is light with the confusion of two things, hunger for you and scare if I am lost. Nothing frights me more than this errand and nothing is more temptation. From the day you disappear I dream and plot. To learn where you are and how to be there. I want to run across the trail through the beech and white pine but I am asking myself which way? Who will tell me? Who lives in the wilderness between this farm and you and will they help me or harm me? What about the boneless bears in the valley? Remember? How when they move their pelts sway as though there is nothing underneath? Their smell belying their beauty, their eyes knowing us from when we are beasts also. You telling me that is why it is fatal to look them in the eye. They will approach, run to us to love and play which we misread and give back fear and anger. Giant birds also are nesting out there bigger than cows, Lina says, and not all natives are like her, she says, so watch out. A praying savage, neighbors call her, because she is once churchgoing yet she bathes herself every day and Christians never do. Underneath she wears bright blue beads and dances in secret at first light when the moon is small. More than fear of loving bears or birds bigger than cows, I fear pathless night. How, I wonder, can I find you in the dark? Now at last there is a way. I have orders. It is arranged. I will see your mouth and trail my fingers down. You will rest your chin in my hair again while I breathe into your shoulder in and out, in and out. I am happy the world is breaking open for us, yet its newness trembles me. To get to you I must leave the only home, the only people I know. Lina says from the state of my teeth I am maybe seven or eight when I am brought here. We boil wild plums for jam and cake eight times since then, so I must be sixteen. Before this place I spend my days picking okra and sweeping tobacco sheds, my nights on the floor of the cookhouse with a

minha mãe. We are baptized and can have happiness
when this life is done. The Reverend Father tells us that.
Once every seven days we learn to read and write. We
are forbidden to leave the place so the four of us hide
near the marsh. My mother, me, her little boy and Reverend Father. He is forbidden to do this but he teaches
us anyway watching out for wicked Virginians and
Protestants who want to catch him. If they do he will be
in prison or pay money or both. He has two books and
a slate. We have sticks to draw through sand, pebbles to
shape words on smooth flat rock. When the letters are
memory we make whole words. I am faster than my
mother and her baby boy is no good at all. Very quickly
I can write from memory the Nicene Creed including
all of the commas. Confession we tell not write as I am
doing now. I forget almost all of it until now. I like talk.
Lina talk, stone talk, even Sorrow talk. Best of all is your
talk. At first when I am brought here I don't talk any
word. All of what I hear is different from what words
mean to a minha mãe and me. Lina's words say nothing
I know. Nor Mistress's. Slowly a little talk is in my
mouth and not on stone. Lina says the place of my talking on stone is Mary's Land where Sir does business. So
that is where my mother and her baby boy are buried.
Or will be if they ever decide to rest. Sleeping on the
cookhouse floor with them is not as nice as sleeping in
the broken sleigh with Lina. In cold weather we put
planks around our part of the cowshed and wrap our
arms together under pelts. We don't smell the cow flops
because they are frozen and we are deep under fur. In
summer if our hammocks are hit by mosquitoes Lina

makes a cool place to sleep out of branches. You never like a hammock and prefer the ground even in rain when Sir offers you the storehouse. Sorrow no more sleeps near the fireplace. The men helping you, Will and Scully, never live the night here because their master does not allow it. You remember them, how they would not take orders from you until Sir makes them? He could do that since they are exchange for land under lease from Sir. Lina says Sir has a clever way of getting without giving. I know it is true because I see it forever and ever. Me watching, my mother listening, her baby boy on her hip. Senhor is not paying the whole amount he owes to Sir. Sir saying he will take instead the woman and the girl, not the baby boy and the debt is gone. A minha mãe begs no. Her baby boy is still at her breast. Take the girl, she says, my daughter, she says. Me. Me. Sir agrees and changes the balance due. As soon as tobacco leaf is hanging to dry Reverend Father takes me on a ferry, then a ketch, then a boat and bundles me between his boxes of books and food. The second day it becomes hurting cold and I am happy I have a cloak however thin. Reverend Father excuses himself to go elsewhere on the boat and tells me to stay exact where I am. A woman comes to me and says stand up. I do and she takes my cloak from my shoulders. Then my wooden shoes. She walks away. Reverend Father turns a pale red color when he returns and learns what happens. He rushes all about asking where and who but can find no answer. Finally he takes rags, strips of sailcloth lying about and wraps my feet. Now I am knowing that unlike with Senhor, priests are unlove here. A sailor spits into the sea when Reverend Father asks him for help. Reverend Father is the only kind man I ever see. When I arrive here I believe it is the place he warns against. The freezing in hell that comes before the everlasting fire where sinners bubble and singe forever. But the ice comes first, he says. And when I see knives of it hanging from the houses and trees and feel the white air burn my face I am certain the fire is coming. Then Lina smiles when she looks at me and wraps me for warmth. Mistress looks away. Nor is Sorrow happy to see me. She flaps her hand in front of her face as though bees are bothering her. She is ever strange and Lina says she is once more with child. Father still not clear and Sorrow does not say. Will and Scully laugh and deny. Lina believes it is Sir's. Says she has her reason for thinking so. When I ask what reason she says he is a man. Mistress says nothing. Neither do I. But I have a worry. Not because our work is more, but because mothers nursing greedy babies scare me. I know how their eyes go when they choose. How they raise them to look at me hard, saying something I cannot hear. Saying something important to me, but holding the little boy's hand.

The man moved through the surf, stepping carefully over pebbles and sand to shore. Fog, Atlantic and reeking of plant life, blanketed the bay and slowed him. He could see his boots sloshing but not his satchel nor his hands. When the surf was behind him and his soles sank in mud, he turned to wave to the sloopmen, but because the mast had disappeared in the fog he could not tell whether they remained anchored or risked sailing on—hugging the shore and approximating the location of wharves and docks. Unlike the English fogs he had known since he could walk, or those way north where he lived now, this one was sun fired, turning the world into thick, hot gold. Penetrating it was like struggling through a dream. As mud became swamp grass, he turned left, stepping gingerly until he stumbled against wooden planks leading up beach toward the village.

Other than his own breath and tread, the world was soundless. It was only after he reached the live oak trees that the fog wavered and split. He moved faster then, more in control but missing, too, the blinding gold he had come through.

Picking his way with growing confidence, he arrived in the ramshackle village sleeping between two huge riverside plantations. There the hostler was persuaded to forgo a deposit if the man signed a note: Jacob Vaark. The saddle was poorly made but the horse, Regina, was a fine one. Mounted, he felt better and rode carefree and a little too fast along beach fronts until he entered an old Lenape trail. Here there was reason to be cautious and he slowed Regina down. In this territory he could not be sure of friend or foe. Half a dozen years ago an army of blacks, natives, whites, mulattoes—freedmen, slaves and indentured—had waged war against local gentry led by members of that very class. When that "people's war" lost its hopes to the hangman, the work it had done—which included the slaughter of opposing tribes and running the Carolinas off their land—spawned a thicket of new laws authorizing chaos in defense of order. By eliminating manumission, gatherings, travel and bearing arms for black people only; by granting license to any white to kill any black for any reason; by compensating owners for a slave's maiming or death, they separated and protected all whites from all others forever. Any social ease between gentry and laborers, forged before and during that rebellion, crumbled beneath a hammer wielded in the interests of the gentry's profits. In Jacob Vaark's view, these were lawless laws encouraging cruelty in exchange for common cause, if not common virtue.

In short, 1682 and Virginia was still a mess. Who could keep up with the pitched battles for God, king and land? Even with the relative safety of his skin, solitary traveling required prudence. He knew he might ride for hours with no company but geese flying over inland waterways, and suddenly, from behind felled trees a starving deserter with a pistol might emerge, or in a hollow a family of runaways might cower, or an armed felon might threaten. Carrying several kinds of specie and a single knife, he was a juicy target. Eager to be out of this colony into a less precarious but personally more repellent one, Jacob urged the mare to a faster pace. He dismounted twice, the second time to free the bloody hindleg of a young raccoon stuck in a tree break. Regina munched trail-side grass while he tried to be as gentle as possible, avoiding the claws and teeth of the frightened animal. Once he succeeded, the raccoon limped off, perhaps to the mother forced to abandon it or more likely into other claws.

Galloping along, he was sweating so heavily his eyes salted and his hair matted on his shoulders. Already October and Regina was drenched and snorting. No such thing as winter down here, he thought, and he might as well have been in Barbados, which he had considered once, although its heat was rumored to be more lethal than this. But that was years ago and the decision was null before he could act on it. An uncle he had never met from the side of his family that had abandoned him died and left him one hundred and twenty acres of a dormant patroonship in a climate he much preferred. One with four distinct seasons. Yet this mist, hot and rife with gnats, did not dampen his spirits. Despite the long sail in three vessels down three different bodies of water, and now the hard ride over the Lenape trail, he took delight in the journey. Breathing the air of a world so new, almost alarming in rawness and temptation, never failed to invigorate him. Once beyond the warm gold of the bay, he saw forests untouched since Noah, shorelines beautiful enough to bring tears, wild food for the taking. The lies of the Company about the easy profit awaiting all comers did not surprise or discourage him. In fact it was hardship, adventure, that attracted him. His whole life had been a mix of confrontation, risk and placating. Now here he was, a ratty orphan become landowner, making a place out of no place, a temperate living from raw life. He relished never knowing what lay in his path, who might approach with what intention. A quick thinker, he flushed with pleasure when a crisis, large or small, needed invention and fast action. Rocking in the poorly made saddle, he faced forward while his eyes swept the surroundings. He knew the landscape intimately from years ago when it was still the old Swedish Nation and, later, when he was an agent for the Company. Still later when the Dutch took control. During and after that contest, there had never been much point in knowing who claimed this or that terrain; this or another outpost. Other than certain natives, to whom it all belonged, from one year to another any stretch might be claimed by a church, controlled by a Company or become the private property of a royal's

gift to a son or a favorite. Since land claims were always
fluid, except for notations on bills of sale, he paid scant
attention to old or new names of towns or forts: Fort
Orange; Cape Henry; Nieuw Amsterdam; Wiltwyck. In
his own geography he was moving from Algonquin to
Sesquehanna via Chesapeake on through Lenape since
turtles had a life span longer than towns. When he sailed
the South River into the Chesapeake Bay, he disem-
barked, found a village and negotiated native trails on
horseback, mindful of their fields of maize, careful
through their hunting grounds, politely asking permission to enter a small village here, a larger one there. He
watered his horse at a particular stream and avoided
threatening marshland fronting the pines. Recognizing
the slope of certain hills, a copse of oak, an abandoned
den, the sudden odor of pine sap—all of that was more
than valuable; it was essential. In such ad hoc territory,
Jacob simply knew that when he came out of that forest
of pine skirting the marshes, he was, at last, in Maryland
which, at the moment, belonged to the king. Entirely.

Upon entering this privately owned country, his feel-
ings fought one another to a draw. Unlike colonies up
and down the coast—disputed, fought over and regularly renamed; their trade limited to whatever nation
was victor—the province of Maryland allowed trade to
foreign markets. Good for planters, better for mer-
chants, best for brokers. But the palatinate was Romish
to the core. Priests strode openly in its towns; their temples menaced its squares; their sinister missions cropped
up at the edge of native villages. Law, courts and trade
were their exclusive domain and overdressed women in

raised heels rode in carts driven by ten-year-old
Negroes. He was offended by the lax, flashy cunning of
the Papists. "Abhor that arrant whore of Rome." The
entire class in the children's quarter of the poorhouse
had memorized those lines from their primer. "And all
her blasphemies / Drink not of her cursed cup / Obey
not her decrees." Which did not mean you could not do
business with them, and he had out-dealt them often
enough, especially here where tobacco and slaves were
married, each currency clutching its partner's elbow. By
sustained violence or sudden disease, either one was
subject to collapse, inconveniencing everybody but the
lender.

Disdain, however difficult to cloak, must be put
aside. His previous dealings with this estate had been
with the owner's clerk while sitting on alehouse stools.
Now, for some reason, he had been invited, summoned
rather, to the planter's house—a plantation called
Jublio. A trader asked to dine with a gentleman? On a
Sunday? So there must be trouble, he thought. Finally,
swatting mosquitoes and on the watch for mud snakes
that startled the horse, he glimpsed the wide iron gates
of Jublio and guided Regina through them. He had
heard how grand it was, but could not have been prepared for what lay before him. The house, honey-
colored stone, was in truth more like a place where one
held court. Far away to the right, beyond the iron fences
enclosing the property and softened by mist, he saw
rows of quarters, quiet, empty. In the fields, he reck-
oned, trying to limit the damage sopping weather had
wrought on the crop. The comfortable smell of tobacco

leaves, like fireplaces and good women serving ale, cloaked Jublio like balm. The path ended at a small brick plaza, announcing a prideful entrance to a veranda. Jacob stopped. A boy appeared and, dismounting a bit stiffly, he handed over the reins, cautioning the boy.

"Water. No feed."

"Yes, sir," said the boy and turned the horse around, murmuring, "Nice lady. Nice lady," as he led her away.

Jacob Vaark climbed three brick steps, then retraced them to stand back from the house and appraise it. Two wide windows, at least two dozen panes in each, flanked the door. Five more windows on a broad second story held sunlight glittering above the mist. He had never seen a house like it. The wealthiest men he knew built in wood, not brick, riven clapboards with no need for grand pillars suitable for a House of Parliament. Grandiose, he thought, but easy, easy to build in that climate. Soft southern wood, creamy stone, no caulking needed, everything designed for breeze, not freeze. Long hall, probably, parlors, chambers . . . easy work, easy living, but, Lord, the heat.

He removed his hat and wiped the sweat from his hairline with his sleeve. Then, fingering his soaking collar, he remounted the steps and tested the boot scraper. Before he could knock, the door was opened by a small, contradictory man: aged and ageless, deferential and mocking, white hair black face.

"Afternoon, sir."

"Mr. Ortega is expecting me." Jacob surveyed the room over the old man's head.

"Yes, sir. Your hat, sir? Senhor D'Ortega is expecting you. Thank you, sir. This way, sir."

Footfalls, loud and aggressive, were followed by D'Ortega's call.

"Well timed! Come, Jacob. Come." He motioned toward a parlor.

"Good day, sir. Thank you, sir," said Jacob, marveling at his host's coat, his stockings, his fanciful wig. Elaborate and binding as those trappings must be in the heat, D'Ortega's skin was as dry as parchment, while Jacob continued to perspire. The condition of the handkerchief he pulled from his pocket embarrassed him as much as his need for it.

Seated at a small table surrounded by graven idols, the windows closed to the boiling air, he drank sassafras beer and agreed with his host about the weather and dismissed his apologies for making him endure it to come all this way. That said, D'Ortega swiftly got to business. Disaster had struck. Jacob had heard about it, but listened politely with a touch of compassion to the version this here client/debtor recounted. D'Ortega's ship had been anchored a nautical mile from shore for a month waiting for a vessel, due any day, to replenish what he had lost. A third of his cargo had died of ship fever. Fined five thousand pounds of tobacco by the Lord Proprietarys' magistrate for throwing their bodies too close to the bay; forced to scoop up the corpses—those they could find (they used pikes and nets, D'Ortega said, a purchase which itself cost two pounds, six)—and ordered to burn or bury them. He'd had to pile them in two drays (six shillings), cart them out to low land where saltweed and alligators would finish the work.

Does he cut his losses and let his ship sail on to Barbados? No, thought Jacob. A sloven man, stubborn in his wrongheadedness like all of the Roman faith, he waits in port for another month for a phantom ship from Lisbon carrying enough cargo to replenish the heads he has lost. While waiting to fill his ship's hold to capacity, it sinks and he has lost not only the vessel, not only the original third, but all, except the crew who were unchained, of course, and four unsalable Angolans red-eyed with anger. Now he wanted more credit and six additional months to pay what he had borrowed.

Dinner was a tedious affair made intolerable by the awkwardness Jacob felt. His rough clothes were in stark contrast to embroidered silk and lace collar. His normally deft fingers turned clumsy with the tableware. There was even a trace of raccoon blood on his hands. Seeded resentment now bloomed. Why such a show on a sleepy afternoon for a single guest well below their station? Intentional, he decided; a stage performance to humiliate him into a groveling acceptance of D'Ortega's wishes. The meal began with a prayer whispered in a language he could not decipher and a slow signing of the cross before and after. In spite of his dirty hands and sweat-limp hair, Jacob pressed down his annoyance and chose to focus on the food. But his considerable hunger shrank when presented with the heavily seasoned dishes: everything except pickles and radishes was fried or overcooked. The wine, watered and too sweet for his taste, disappointed him, and the company got worse. The sons were as silent as tombs. D'Ortega's wife was a chattering magpie, asking pointless questions—How do you manage living in snow?—and making sense-defying observations, as though her political judgment were equal to a man's. Perhaps it was their pronunciation, their narrow grasp of the English language, but it seemed to Jacob that nothing transpired in the conversation that had footing in the real world. They both spoke of the gravity, the unique responsibility, this untamed world offered them; its unbreakable connection to God's work and the difficulties they endured on His behalf. Caring for ill or recalcitrant labor was enough, they said, for canonization.

"Are they often ill, Madam?" asked Jacob.

"As they pretend, no," said his hostess. "Scoundrels they are. In Portugal they never get away with this trickery."

"They come from Portugal?" Jacob wondered if the serving woman understood English or if they cursed her only in Portuguese.

"Well, the Angola part of Portugal," said D'Ortega. "It is the most amiable, beautiful land."

"Portugal?"

"Angola. But, of course, Portugal is without peer."

"We are there for four years," added Mistress D'Ortega.

"Portugal?"

"Angola. But, mind you, our children are not born there."

"Portugal, then?"

"No. Maryland."

"Ah. England."

As it turned out, D'Ortega was the third son of a cattleman, in line for nothing. He'd gone to Angola, Portugal's slave pool, to manage shipments to Brazil, but found promises of wealth quicker and more generously met farther abroad. The kick up from one kind of herding to another was swift and immensely enriching. For a while, thought Jacob. D'Ortega did not seem to be making a go of his relatively new station, but he had no doubt he would prevail somehow, as this invitation to dinner was designed to prove.

They had six children, two of whom were old enough to sit at table. Stone-quiet boys, thirteen and fourteen, wearing periwigs like their father as though they were at a ball or a court of law. His bitterness, Jacob understood, was unworthy, the result of having himself no survivors—male or otherwise. Now that his daughter Patrician had followed her dead brothers, there was no one yet to reap the modest but respectable inheritance he hoped to accumulate. Thus, tamping envy as taught in the poorhouse, Jacob entertained himself by conjuring up flaws in the couple's marriage. They seemed well suited to each other: vain, voluptuous, prouder of their pewter and porcelain than of their sons. It was abundantly clear why D'Ortega was in serious debt. Turning profit into useless baubles, unembarrassed by sumptuary, silk stockings and an overdressed wife, wasting candles in midday, he would always be unable to ride out any setback, whether it be lost ship or ruined crop. Watching the couple, Jacob noticed that husband and wife never looked at each other, except for a stolen glance when the other looked elsewhere. He could not tell what was in those surreptitious peeks, but it amused him to divine the worst while he endured the foolish, incomprehensible talk and inedible dishes. They did not smile, they sneered; did not laugh, giggled. He imagined them vicious with servants and obsequious to priests. His initial embarrassment about the unavoidable consequences of his long journey—muddy boots, soiled hands, perspiration and its odor—was dimmed by Mistress D'Ortega's loud perfume and heavily powdered face. The only, if minor, relief came from the clove-smelling woman who brought the food.

His own Rebekka seemed ever more valuable to him the rare times he was in the company of these rich men's wives, women who changed frocks every day and dressed their servants in sacking. From the moment he saw his bride-to-be struggling down the gangplank with bedding, two boxes and a heavy satchel, he knew his good fortune. He had been willing to accept a bag of bones or an ugly maiden—in fact expected one, since a pretty one would have had several local opportunities to wed. But the young woman who answered his shout in the crowd was plump, comely and capable. Worth every day of the long search made necessary because taking over the patroonship required a wife, and because he wanted a certain kind of mate: an unchurched woman of childbearing age, obedient but not groveling, literate but not proud, independent but nurturing. And he would accept no scold. Just as the first mate's report described her, Rebekka was ideal. There was not a shrewish bone in her body. She never raised her voice in anger. Saw to his needs, made the tenderest dumplings, took to chores in a land completely strange to her with enthusiasm and invention, cheerful as a bluebird. Or used to be. Three dead infants in a row, followed by the accidental death of Patrician, their five-year-old, had unleavened her. A kind of invisible ash had settled over her which vigils at the small graves in the meadow did nothing to wipe away. Yet she neither complained nor shirked her duties. If anything, she threw herself more vigorously into the farmwork, and when he traveled, as now, on business, trading, collecting, lending, he had no doubts about how his home was being managed. Rebekka and her two helpers were as reliable as sunrise and strong as posts. Besides, time and health were on their side. He was confident she would bear more children and at least one, a boy, would live to thrive.

Dessert, applesauce and pecans, was an improvement, and when he accompanied D'Ortega on the impossible-to-refuse tour of the place, his mood had lifted slightly, enough to admire the estate honestly. The mist had cleared and he was able to see in detail the workmanship and care of the tobacco sheds, wagons, row after row of barrels—orderly and nicely kept—the well-made meat house, milk house, laundry, cookhouse. All but the last, whitewashed plaster, a jot smaller than the slave quarters but, unlike them, in excellent repair. The subject, the purpose, of the meeting had not been approached. D'Ortega had described with attention to minute detail the accidents beyond his control that made him unable to pay what he owed. But how Jacob would be reimbursed had not been broached. Examining the spotted, bug-ridden leaves of tobacco, it became clear what D'Ortega had left to offer. Slaves.

Jacob refused. His farm was modest; his trade needed

only himself. Besides having no place to put them, there was nothing to occupy them.

"Ridiculous," said D'Ortega. "You sell them. Do you know the prices they garner?"

Jacob winced. Flesh was not his commodity.

Still, at his host's insistence, he trailed him to the little sheds where D'Ortega interrupted their half day's rest and ordered some two dozen or more to assemble in a straight line, including the boy who had watered Regina. The two men walked the row, inspecting. D'Ortega identifying talents, weaknesses and possibilities, but silent about the scars, the wounds like misplaced veins tracing their skin. One even had the facial brand required by local law when a slave assaulted a white man a second time. The women's eyes looked shockproof, gazing beyond place and time as though they were not actually there. The men looked at the ground. Except every now and then, when possible, when they thought they were not being evaluated, Jacob could see their quick glances, sideways, wary but, most of all, judging the men who judged them.

Suddenly Jacob felt his stomach seize. The tobacco odor, so welcoming when he arrived, now nauseated him. Or was it the sugared rice, the hog cuts fried and dripping with molasses, the cocoa Lady D'Ortega was giddy about? Whatever it was, he couldn't stay there surrounded by a passel of slaves whose silence made him imagine an avalanche seen from a great distance. No sound, just the knowledge of a roar he could not hear. He begged off, saying the proposal was not acceptable— too much trouble to transport, manage, auction; his solitary, unencumbered proficiency was what he liked about trade. Specie, bills of credit, quit claims, were portable. One satchel carried all he needed. They walked back toward the house and through the side gate in the ornate fence, D'Ortega pontificating all the while. He would do the selling. Pounds? Spanish sovereigns? He would arrange transportation, hire the handler.

Stomach turning, nostrils assailed, Jacob grew angry. This is a calamity, he thought. Unresolved, it would lead to years in a lawsuit in a province ruled by the king's judges disinclined to favor a distant tradesman over a local Catholic gentleman. The loss, while not unmanageable, struck him as unforgivable. And to such a man. D'Ortega's strut as they had walked the property disgusted him. Moreover, he believed the set of that jaw, the drooping lids, hid something soft, as if his hands, accustomed to reins, whips and lace, had never held a plow or axed a tree. There was something beyond Catholic in him, something sordid and overripe. But what could he do? Jacob felt the shame of his weakened position like a soiling of the blood. No wonder they had been excluded from Parliament back home and, although he did not believe they should be hunted down like vermin, other than on business he would never choose to mingle or socialize with the lowest or highest of them. Barely listening to D'Ortega's patter, sly, indirect, instead of straight and manly, Jacob neared the cookhouse and saw a woman standing in the doorway with two children. One on her hip; one hiding behind her skirts. She looked healthy enough, better fed than the others. On a whim, mostly to silence him and fairly sure D'Ortega would refuse, he said, "Her. That one. I'll take her."

D'Ortega stopped short, a startled look on his face. "Ah, no. Impossible. My wife won't allow. She can't live without her. She is our main cook, the best one."

Jacob drew closer and, recognizing the clove-laced sweat, suspected there was more than cooking D'Ortega stood to lose.

"You said 'any.' I could choose any. If your word is worthless, there is only the law."

D'Ortega lifted an eyebrow, just one, as though on its curve an empire rested. Jacob knew he was struggling with this impertinent threat from an inferior, but he must have thought better of returning the insult with another. He desperately wanted this business over quickly and he wanted his way.

"Well, yes," said D'Ortega, "but there are other women here. More. You see them. Also this one is nursing."

"Then the law it is," said Jacob.

D'Ortega smiled. A lawsuit would certainly be decided in his favor and the time wasted in pursuing it would be to his advantage.

"You astound me," he said.

Jacob refused to back down. "Perhaps another lender would be more to your liking," he said and enjoyed seeing the nostril flare that meant he had struck home. D'Ortega was notorious for unpaid debts and had to search far outside Maryland for a broker since he had exhausted his friends and local lenders refused what they knew would be inevitable default. The air tightened.

"You don't seem to comprehend my offer. I not forfeiting my debt. I honoring it. The value of a seasoned slave is beyond adequate."

"Not if I can't use her."

"Use her? Sell her!"

"My trade is goods and gold, sir," said Jacob Vaark, landowner. And he could not resist adding, "But I understand how hard it is for a Papist to accommodate certain kinds of restraint."

Too subtle? wondered Jacob. Not at all, apparently, for D'Ortega's hand moved to his hip. Jacob's eyes followed the movement as the ringed fingers curled around a scabbard. Would he? Would this curdled, arrogant fop really assault his creditor, murder him and, claiming self-defense, prerogative, rid himself of both debt and social insult even though it would mean complete financial disaster, considering that his coffers were as empty as his scabbard? The soft fingers fumbled for the absent haft. Jacob raised his eyes to D'Ortega's, noticing the cowardice of unarmed gentry confronted with a commoner. Out here in wilderness dependent on paid guards nowhere in sight this Sunday. He felt like laughing. Where else but in this disorganized world would such an encounter be possible? Where else could rank tremble before courage? Jacob turned away, letting his exposed, unarmed back convey his scorn. It was a curious moment. Along with his contempt, he felt a wave of exhilaration. Potent. Steady. An inside shift from careful negotiator to the raw boy that once prowled the lanes of town and country. He did not even try to mute his chuckling as he passed the cookhouse and glanced again at the woman standing in its door.

Just then the little girl stepped from behind the mother. On her feet was a pair of way-too-big woman's shoes. Perhaps it was that feeling of license, a newly recovered recklessness along with the sight of those little legs rising like two bramble sticks from the bashed and broken shoes, that made him laugh. A loud, chest-heaving laugh at the comedy, the hopeless irritation, of the visit. His laughter had not subsided when the woman cradling the small boy on her hip came forward. Her voice was barely above a whisper but there was no mistaking its urgency.

"Please, Senhor. Not me. Take her. Take my daughter."

Jacob looked up at her, away from the child's feet, his mouth still open with laughter, and was struck by the terror in her eyes. His laugh creaking to a close, he shook his head, thinking, God help me if this is not the most wretched business.

"Why yes. Of course," said D'Ortega, shaking off his earlier embarrassment and trying to re-establish his dignity. "I'll send her to you. Immediately." His eyes widened as did his condescending smile, though he still seemed highly agitated.

"My answer is firm," said Jacob, thinking, I've got to get away from this substitute for a man. But thinking also, perhaps Rebekka would welcome a child around the place. This one here, swimming in horrible shoes, appeared to be about the same age as Patrician, and if she got kicked in the head by a mare, the loss would not rock Rebekka so.

"There is a priest here," D'Ortega went on. "He can

bring her to you. I'll have them board a sloop to any port on the coast you desire. . . ."

"No. I said, no."

Suddenly the woman smelling of cloves knelt and closed her eyes.

They wrote new papers. Agreeing that the girl was worth twenty pieces of eight, considering the number of years ahead of her and reducing the balance by three hogsheads of tobacco or fifteen English pounds, the latter preferred. The tension lifted, visibly so on D'Ortega's face. Eager to get away and re-nourish his good opinion of himself, Jacob said abrupt goodbyes to Mistress D'Ortega, the two boys and their father. On his way to the narrow track, he turned Regina around, waved at the couple and once again, in spite of himself, envied the house, the gate, the fence. For the first time he had not tricked, not flattered, not manipulated, but gone head to head with rich gentry. And realized, not for the first time, that only things, not bloodlines or character, separated them. So mighten it be nice to have such a fence to enclose the headstones in his own meadow? And one day, not too far away, to build a house that size on his own property? On that rise in back, with a better prospect of the hills and the valley between them? Not as ornate as D'Ortega's. None of that pagan excess, of course, but fair. And pure, noble even, because it would not be compromised as Jublio was. Access to a fleet of free labor made D'Ortega's leisurely life possible. Without a shipload of enslaved Angolans he would not be merely in debt; he would be eating from his palm instead of porcelain and sleeping in the bush of Africa rather than a four-post bed. Jacob sneered at wealth dependent on a captured workforce that required more force to maintain. Thin as they were, the dregs of his kind of Protestantism recoiled at whips, chains and armed overseers. He was determined to prove that his own industry could amass the fortune, the station, D'Ortega claimed without trading his conscience for coin.

He tapped Regina to a faster pace. The sun was low; the air cooler. He was in a hurry to get back into Virginia, its shore, and to Pursey's tavern before night, sleep in a bed if they weren't all packed three or four abreast. Otherwise he would join the other patrons and curl on any surface. But first he would have one, perhaps two, drafts of ale, its bitter, clear taste critical to eliminating the sweetish rot of vice and ruined tobacco that seemed to coat his tongue. Jacob returned Regina to the hostler, paid him and strolled to the wharf and Pursey's tavern. On the way he saw a man beating a horse to its knees. Before he could open his mouth to shout, rowdy sailors pulled the man away and let him feel his own knees in mud. Few things angered Jacob more than the brutal handling of domesticated animals. He did not know what the sailors were objecting to, but his own fury was not only because of the pain it inflicted on the horse, but because of the mute, unprotesting surrender glazing its eyes.

Pursey's was closed on Sunday, as he should have known, so he went to the one always open. Rough, illegal and catering to hard boys, it nevertheless offered good, plentiful food and never strong meat. On his sec-

ond draft, a fiddler and a piper entered for their merri-
ment and their money and, the piper having played less
well than himself, raised Jacob's spirits enough for him
to join in the singing. When two women came in, the
men called out their names with liquored glee. The
bawds flounced a bit before choosing a lap to sit in.
Jacob demurred when approached. He'd had enough,
years ago, of brothels and the disorderly houses kept by
wives of sailors at sea. The boyish recklessness that
flooded him at Jublio did not extend to the sweet
debauchery he had sought as a youth.

Seated at a table cluttered with the remains of earlier
meals, he listened to the talk around him, which was
mostly sugar, which was to say, rum. Its price and
demand becoming greater than tobacco's now that glut
was ruining that market. The man who seemed to know
most about kill-devil, the simple mechanics of its pro-
duction, its outrageous prices and beneficial effects, was
holding forth with the authority of a mayor.

Burly, pock-faced, he had the aura of a man who had
been in exotic places and the eyes of someone unaccus-
tomed to looking at things close to his face. Downes was
his name. Peter Downes. A Negro boy had been summoned and now brought six tankards, the handles of
three in each hand, and set them on the table. Five men
reached for them and quickly swallowed. Downes also,
but spit his first swallow on the floor, telling the company that the gesture was both an offering and a protection from poison.

"How so?" someone asked. "Poison may lurk at the
bottom."

"Never," said Downes. "Poison is like the drowned; it always floats."

Amid the laughter, Jacob joined the men at the table and listened to Downes' mesmerizing tales ending with a hilarious description of the size of the women's breasts in Barbados.

"I once thought of settling there," said Jacob. "Besides bosoms, what is it like?"

"Like a whore. Lush and deadly," said Downes.

"Meaning?"

Downes wiped his lips with his sleeve. "Meaning all is plentiful and ripe except life. That is scarce and short. Six months, eighteen and—" He waved goodbye fingers.

"Then how do they manage? It must be constant turmoil." Jacob was imagining the difference between the steady controlled labor of Jublio and the disorderliness of sugar plantations.

"Not at all," Downes smiled. "They ship in more. Like firewood, what burns to ash is refueled. And don't forget, there are births. The place is a stew of mulattoes, creoles, zambos, mestizos, lobos, chinos, coyotes." He touched his fingers with his thumb as he listed the types being produced in Barbados.

"Still the risk is high," countered Jacob. "I've heard of whole estates cut down by disease. What will happen when labor dwindles and there is less and less to transport?"

"Why would it dwindle?" Downes spread his hands as if carrying the hull of a ship. "Africans are as interested in selling slaves to the Dutch as an English planter is in buying them. Rum rules, no matter who does the trading. Laws? What laws? Look," he went on, "Massachusetts has already tried laws against rum selling and failed to stop one dram. The sale of molasses to northern colonies is brisker than ever. More steady profit in it than fur, tobacco, lumber, anything—except gold, I reckon. As long as the fuel is replenished, vats simmer and money heaps. Kill-devil, sugar—there will never be enough. A trade for lifetimes to come."

"Still," Jacob said, "it's a degraded business. And hard."

"Think of it this way. Fur you need to hunt it, kill it, skin it, carry it and probably fight some natives for the rights. Tobacco needs nurture, harvest, drying, packing, toting, but mostly time and ever-fresh soil. Sugar? Rum? Cane grows. You can't stop it; its soil never dies out. You just cut it, cook it, ship it." Downes slapped his palms together.

"That simple, eh?"

"More or less. But the point is this. No loss of investment. None. Ever. No crop failure. No wiped-out beaver or fox. No war to interfere. Crop plentiful, eternal. Slave workers, same. Buyers, eager. Product, heavenly. In a month, the time of the journey from mill to Boston, a man can turn fifty pounds into five times as much. Think of it. Each and every month five times the investment. For certain."

Jacob had to laugh. He recognized the manner: hawker turned middle man eliminating all hesitations and closing all arguments with promises of profit quickly. From Downes' clothes and his apparent unwillingness so far to stand the drinks, Jacob suspected he had not reaped the easy profit he described.

Nevertheless, Jacob decided he would look into it.

After a leisurely meal of oysters, veal, pigeon, parsnips and suet pudding restored his taste buds, he reserved bed space with just one man in it and, strolling outside, thought about the disappointing day and the humiliation of having accepted the girl as part payment. He knew he would never see another farthing from D'Ortega. One day—soon, maybe—to everyone's relief the Stuarts would lose the throne, and a Protestant rule. Then, he thought, a case against D'Ortega would succeed and he would not be forced to settle for a child as a percentage of what was due him. He knew he had excused the bargain by thinking Rebekka would be eager to have her, but what was truer than that was another thing. From his own childhood he knew there was no good place in the world for waifs and whelps other than the generosity of strangers. Even if bartered, given away, apprenticed, sold, swapped, seduced, tricked for food, labored for shelter or stolen, they were less doomed under adult control. Even if they mattered less than a milch cow to a parent or master, without an adult they were more likely to freeze to death on stone steps, float facedown in canals, or wash up on banks and shoals. He refused to be sentimental about his own orphan status, the years spent with children of all shades, stealing food and cadging gratuities for errands. His mother, he was told, was a girl of no consequence who died in childbirth. His father, who hailed from Amsterdam, left him with a name easily punned and a cause of deep suspicion. The shame the Dutch had visited on the English was everywhere, especially during his stint in a poorhouse before the luck of being taken on as a runner for a law firm. The job required literacy and led to his being signed up by the Company. Inheriting land softened the chagrin of being both misborn and disowned. Yet he continued to feel a disturbing pulse of pity for orphans and strays, remembering well their and his own sad teeming in the markets, lanes, alleyways and ports of every region he traveled. Once before he found it hard to refuse when called on to rescue an unmoored, unwanted child. A decade ago now, a sawyer asked him to take off his hands a sullen, curly-headed girl he had found half dead on a riverbank. Jacob agreed to do it, provided the sawyer forgive the cost of the lumber he was buying. Unlike now, at that time his farm really did need more help. Rebekka was pregnant then, but no previous sons had lived. His farm was sixty cultivated acres out of one hundred and twenty of woodland that was located some seven miles from a hamlet founded by Separatists. The patroonship had lain dormant for years when so many Dutch (except for the powerful and wealthy ones) left or were expelled from the region. The land was still isolated except for the Separatists. Jacob soon learned that they had bolted from their brethren over the question of the Chosen versus the universal nature of salvation. His neighbors favored the first and situated themselves inland beyond fur posts and wars. When Jacob, a small-scale trader for the Company with a side line in fur and lumber, found himself an heir of sorts, he relished the thought of becoming a landowning, independent farmer. He didn't change his mind about that. He did what was necessary: secured a wife, someone to help her, planted, built, fathered. . . . He had simply added the trading life. Otherwise he would have to prefer settled farm life and communion with people whose religion dumbfounded him although the seven-mile distance made their blasphemy irrelevant. Yet his land belonged to a traveling man who knew very well that it was not wise to have male labor all over the place during his long absences. His preference for steady female labor over dodgy males was based on his own experience as a youth. A frequently absent master was invitation and temptation—to escape, rape or rob. The two men he used as occasional help presented no threat at all. In the right environment, women were naturally reliable. He believed it now with this ill-shod child that the mother was throwing away, just as he believed it a decade earlier with the curly-haired goose girl, the one they called Sorrow. And the acquisition of both could be seen as rescue. Only Lina had been purchased outright and deliberately, but she was a woman, not a child.

Walking in the warm night air, he went as far as possible, until the alehouse lights were gem stones fighting darkness and the voices of carousing men were lost to the silk-rustle of surf. The sky had forgotten completely its morning fire and was tricked out in cool stars on a canvas smooth and dark as Regina's hide. He gazed at the occasional dapple of starlight on the water, then bent down and placed his hands in it. Sand moved under his palms; infant waves died above his wrists, soaking the cuffs of his sleeves. By and by the detritus of the day washed off, including the faint trace of coon's blood. As he walked back to the inn, nothing was in his way. There was the heat, of course, but no fog, gold or gray, impeded him. Besides, a plan was taking shape. Knowing full well his shortcomings as a farmer—in fact his boredom with its confinement and routine—he had found commerce more to his taste. Now he fondled the idea of an even more satisfying enterprise. And the plan was as sweet as the sugar on which it was based. And there was a profound difference between the intimacy of slave bodies at Jublio and a remote labor force in Barbados. Right? Right, he thought, looking at a sky vulgar with stars. Clear and right. The silver that glittered there was not at all unreachable. And that wide swath of cream pouring through the stars was his for the tasting.

The heat was still pressing, his bed partner overactive, yet he slept well enough. Probably because his dreams were of a grand house of many rooms rising on a hill above the fog.

Since your leaving with no goodbye, summer passes, then autumn, and with the waning of winter the sickness comes back. Not like before with Sorrow but now with Sir. When he returns this time he is different, slow and hard to please. He is short with Mistress. He sweats and wants cider all the time and no one believes the blisters are going to be Sorrow's old sickness. He vomits at night and curses in the day. Then he is too weak to do either. He reminds us that he has chosen help, including me, who are survivors of measles, so how is this happening to him? He cannot help envying our health and feeling the cheat of his new house. I can tell you that even yet it is not complete though your ironwork is wondrous to see. The glittering cobras still kiss at the gate's crown. The house is mighty, waiting only for a glazier. Sir wants to be taken there even though there is no furniture. He tells Mistress to hurry hurry never mind the spring rain pouring down for days. The sickness alters his mind as well as his face. Will and Scully are gone and when we women each holding a corner of a blanket carry him into the house he is sleeping with his mouth wide open and never wakes. Neither Mistress nor we know if he is alive for even one minute to smell the new cherrywood floors he lies on. We are alone. No one to shroud or mourn Sir but us. Will and Scully must sneak to dig the grave. They are warn to stay away. I don't think they wish to. I think their master makes them, because of the sickness. The deacon does not come even though he is a friend who likes Sorrow. Neither do any of the congregation. Still, we do not say the word aloud until we bury him next to his children and Mistress notices two in her mouth. That is the one time we whisper it. Pox. After we say it the next morning, the two on her tongue are joined by twenty-three on her face. Twenty-five in all. She wants you here as much as I do. For her it is to save her life. For me it is to have one.

You probably don't know anything at all about what your back looks like whatever the sky holds: sunlight, moonrise. I rest there. My hand, my eyes, my mouth. The first time I see it you are shaping fire with bellows. The shine of water runs down your spine and I have shock at myself for wanting to lick there. I run away into the cowshed to stop this thing from happening inside me. Nothing stops it. There is only you. Nothing outside of you. My eyes not my stomach are the hungry parts of me. There will never be enough time to look how you move. Your arm goes up to strike iron. You drop to one knee. You bend. You stop to pour water first on the iron then down your throat. Before you know I am in the world I am already kill by you. My mouth is open, my legs go softly and the heart is stretching to break.

Night comes and I steal a candle. I carry an ember in a pot to light it. To see more of you. When it is lit I shield the flame with my hand. I watch you sleeping. I watch too long. Am careless. The flame burns my palm. I think if you wake and see me seeing you I will die. I run away not knowing then you are seeing me seeing you. And when at last our eyes hit I am not dead. For the first time I am live.

Lina twitchy as fresh-hook salmon waits with me in the village. The wagon of the Ney brothers does not come. Hours we stand then sit roadside. A boy and a dog drive goats past us. He raises his hat. That is the first time any male does it to me. I like it. A good sign I am thinking but Lina is warning me of many things, saying if you are not in your place I must not tarry. I must return at once. I cannot handle a horse so I must seek return on the next day's horse cart, the one that hauls fresh milk and eggs to market. Some people go by and look but do not speak. We are female so they have no fright. They know who is Lina yet look as if we are strange to them. We wait more and so long that I do not save my bread and codfish. I eat all the cod. Lina holds her forehead in her hand, her elbow on her knee. She gives off a bad feeling so I keep my thoughts on the goatherd's hat.

The wind is chill and smells of snow. At last the

wagon is here. I climb up. The driver helps me, stays his hand hard and long on my back parts. I feel shame. We are seven, apart from the brothers Ney, and the horses are not the only ones made nervous by snowflakes in springtime. Their haunches tremble, they shake their manes. We are nervous also but we sit still as the flakes come down and stick to our shawls and hats, sugaring our eyelashes and flouring the men's woolly beards. Two women face into the wind that whips their hair like corn tassel, their eyes slits of shine. The other one covers her mouth with her cloak and leans against a man. A boy with a yellow pigtail sits on the wagon floor, his hands tied to his ankles. He and I are the only ones without rugs or blankets covering our feet.

Sudden snowfall on tender leaves is pretty. Perhaps it will last long enough on the ground to make animal tracking easy. Men are always happy in the snow where killing is best. Sir says no one can starve if there is snow. Nor in spring because even before berries are out and vegetables ready to eat the river is full of spawn and the air of fowl. But this snow will not last, although it is heavy, wet and thick. I draw my feet under my skirt, not for warmth, but to protect the letter. The cloth of bread I clutch on my lap.

Mistress makes me memorize the way to get to you. I am to board the Ney brothers' wagon in the morning as it travels north on the post road. After one stop at a tavern, the wagon will arrive at a place she calls Hartkill just after midday where I disembark. I am to walk left, westward on the Abenaki trail which I will know by the sapling bent into the earth with one sprout growing skyward. But the Ney brothers' wagon is too much late. By the time I climb aboard and take a place at the tail behind the others it is already late afternoon. The others do not ask me where I am heading but after a while are pleasing themselves to whisper where they once live. By the sea, the women say, they cleaning ships, the men caulking them and repairing docks. They are certain their years of debt are over but the master says no. He sends them away, north, to another place, a tannery, for more years. I don't understand why they are sad. Everyone has to work. I ask are you leaving someone dear behind? All heads turn toward me and the wind dies. Daft, a man says. A woman across from me says, young. The man says, same. Another woman raises her voice to say leave her be. Too loud. Settle down back there, the driver is shouting. The one who says I am daft bends down to scratch his ankle, scratching for a long time while the others cough and scrape their shoes as if to defy the driver's command. The woman next to me whispers, there are no coffins in a tannery, only fast death in acid.

The tavern needs lamplight when we reach it. At first I don't see it, but one of us points and then we all do. A light winking through the trees. The Neys go in. We wait. They come out to water the horses and us and go in again. After that there are scuffling sounds again. I look down and see the rope that falls from their ankles twist along the wagon bed. The snow ends and the sun is gone. Quiet, quiet six drop down, the men catching the women in their arms. The boy jumps alone. The three women motion to me. My heart turns over and I drop down too. They move off back down where we are coming from, stepping as best they can figure in tree shelter at roadside, places where the snow is small. I don't follow. Neither can I stay in the wagon. I have a cold stone in my chest. I don't need Lina to warn me that I must not be alone with strange men with slow hands when in liquor and anger they discover their cargo is lost. I have to choose quick. I choose you. I go west into the trees. Everything I want is west. You. Your talk. The medicine you know that will make Mistress well. You will hear what I have to say and come back with me. I have only to go west. One day? Two nights?

I am walking among chestnut trees lining the road. Some already showing leaf hold their breath until the snow melts. The silly ones let their buds drop to the ground like dry peas. I am moving north where the sapling bends into the earth with a sprout that points to the sky. Then west to you. I am hurrying to gain ground before all light is over. The land slopes sharply and I have no way to go but down as well. Hard as I try I lose the road. Tree leaves are too new for shelter, so everywhere the ground is slop with snow and my footprints slide and pool. The sky is the color of currants. Can I go more, I wonder. Should I. Two hares freeze before bounding away. I don't know how to read that. I hear water running and move in the dark toward the sound. The moonlight is young. I hold one arm out in front and go slow to not stumble and fall. But the sound is pines dripping and there is no brook or stream. I make a cup of my hand to get a little fallen snow to swallow. I do not hear the paws or see any shape. It is the smell of wet fur that stops me. If I am smelling it, it is smelling me, because there is nothing with odor left in my food cloth, only bread. I cannot tell if it is bigger than me or smaller or if it is alone. I decide for stillness. I never hear it go but the odor fades at last. I think it is better to climb a tree. The old pines are very big. Any one is good cover even though it tears and fights me. Its branches sway but do not break under me. I hide from everything of creep and slouch. I know sleep will not claim me because I have too much fear. The branches creak and bend. My plan for this night is not good. I need Lina to say how to shelter in wilderness.

Lina was unimpressed by the festive mood, the jittery satisfaction of everyone involved, and had refused to enter or go near it. That third and presumably final house that Sir insisted on building distorted sunlight and required the death of fifty trees. And now having died in it he will haunt its rooms forever. The first house Sir built—dirt floor, green wood—was weaker than the bark-covered one she herself was born in. The second one was strong. He tore down the first to lay wooden floors in the second with four rooms, a decent fireplace and windows with good tight shutters. There was no need for a third. Yet at the very moment when there were no children to occupy or inherit it, he meant to build another, bigger, double-storied, fenced and gated like the one he saw on his travels. Mistress had sighed and confided to Lina that at the least the doing of it would keep him more on the land.

"Trading and traveling fill his pockets," she'd said, "but he had been content to be a farmer when we married. Now . . ." Her voice trailed off as she yanked out the swan's feathers.

During its construction, however, Mistress couldn't keep a smile off her face. Like everyone else, Willard, Scully, hired help, deliverymen, she was happy, cooking as though it were harvest time. Stupid Sorrow gaping with pleasure; the smithy laughing; Florens mindless as fern in wind. And Sir—she had never seen him in better spirits. Not with the birth of his doomed sons, nor with his pleasure in his daughter, not even with an especially successful business arrangement he bragged about. It was not a sudden change, yet it was a deep one. The last few years he seemed moody, less gentle, but when he decided to kill the trees and replace them with a profane monument to himself, he was cheerful every waking moment.

Killing trees in that number, without asking their permission, of course his efforts would stir up malfortune. Sure enough, when the house was close to completion he fell sick with nothing else on his mind. He mystified Lina. All Europes did. Once they terrified her, then they rescued her. Now they simply puzzled her. Why, she wondered, had Mistress sent a love-disabled girl to find the blacksmith? Why not tamp down her pride and seek out one of the Anabaptists? The deacon would be more than willing. Poor Florens, thought Lina. If she is not stolen or murdered, if she finds him safe she would not return. Why should she? Lina had watched first with mild amusement, then with increasing distress the courtship that began the morning the blacksmith came to work on Sir's foolish house. Florens had stood still, a startled doe, when he dismounted his horse, doffed his hat and asked if this was the Vaark place. Lina had shifted the milk bucket to her left hand and pointed up the hill. Mistress, leading the heifer, had come around the corner of the shed and asked him his business, sucking her teeth when he answered.

"Dear Lord," she murmured and, pushing out her bottom lip, blew hair away from her forehead. Then, "Wait here a moment."

As Mistress led the cow to pasture the blacksmith locked eyes with Lina before returning his hat to his head. He never once looked at Florens standing nearby, not breathing, holding the milking stool with both hands as though to help gravity keep her earthbound. She should have known then what the consequences would be, but felt sure that Sorrow, always an easy harvest, would quickly draw his attention and thwart Florens' drooling. Learning from Mistress that he was a free man doubled her anxiety. He had rights, then, and privileges, like Sir. He could marry, own things, travel, sell his own labor. She should have seen the danger immediately because his arrogance was clear. When Mistress returned, rubbing her hands on her apron, he removed his hat once more, then did something Lina had never seen an African do: he looked directly at Mistress, lowering his glance, for he was very tall, never blinking those eyes slanted and yellow as a ram's. It was not true, then, what she had heard; that for them only children and loved ones could be looked in the eye; for all others it was disrespect or a threat. In the town Lina had been taken to, after the conflagration had wiped away her village, that kind of boldness from any African was legitimate cause for a whip. An unfathomable puzzle. Europes could calmly cut mothers down, blast old men in the face with muskets louder than moose calls, but were enraged if a not-Europe looked a Europe in the eye. On the one hand they would torch your home; on the other they would feed, nurse and bless you. Best to judge them one at a time, proof being that one, at least, could become your friend, which is why she slept on the floor beside Mistress' bed and kept watch in case Sorrow came close or Mistress needed something.

Once, long ago, had Lina been older or tutored in healing, she might have eased the pain of her family and all the others dying around her: on mats of rush, lapping at the lake's shore, curled in paths within the village and in the forest beyond, but most tearing at blankets they could neither abide nor abandon. Infants fell silent first, and even as their mothers heaped earth over their bones, they too were pouring sweat and limp as maize hair. At first they fought off the crows, she and two young boys, but they were no match for the birds or the smell, and when the wolves arrived, all three scrambled as high into a beech tree as they could. They stayed there all night listening to gnawing, baying, growling, fighting and worst of all the quiet of animals sated at last. At dawn none of them dared to apply a name to the pieces hauled away from a body or left to insect life. By noon, just as they had decided to make a run for one of the canoes moored in the lake, men in blue uniforms came, their faces wrapped in rags. News of the deaths that had swept her village had reached out. Lina's joy at being rescued collapsed when the soldiers, having taken one look

at the crows and vultures feeding on the corpses strewn
about, shot the wolves then circled the whole village
with fire. As the carrion flew off she did not know
whether to stay hidden or risk being shot as well. But
the boys screamed from the branches until the men
heard them and caught each in their arms as they
jumped, saying *"Calme, mes petits. Calme."* If they worried that the little survivors would infect them, they
chose to ignore it, being true soldiers, unwilling to
slaughter small children.

She never learned where they took the boys, but she
was taken to live among kindly Presbyterians. They were
pleased to have her, they said, because they admired
native women who, they said, worked as hard as they
themselves did, but scorned native men who simply
fished and hunted like gentry all day. Impoverished gentry, that is, since they owned nothing, certainly not the
land they slept on, preferring to live as entitled paupers.
And since some of the church elders had heard horrible
tales of, or witnessed themselves, God's wrath toward
the idle and profane—flinging black death followed by
raging fire on the proud and blasphemous city of their
birth—they could only pray that Lina's people understood before they died that what had befallen them was
merely the first sign of His displeasure: a pouring out of
one of the seven vials, the final one of which would
announce His arrival and the birth of young Jerusalem.
They named her Messalina, just in case, but shortened it
to Lina to signal a sliver of hope. Afraid of once more
losing shelter, terrified of being alone in the world without family, Lina acknowledged her status as heathen and
let herself be purified by these worthies. She learned that

bathing naked in the river was a sin; that plucking cherries from a tree burdened with them was theft; that to
eat corn mush with one's fingers was perverse. That God
hated idleness most of all, so staring off into space to
weep for a mother or a playmate was to court damna-
tion. Covering oneself in the skin of beasts offended
God, so they burned her deerskin dress and gave her a
good duffel cloth one. They clipped the beads from her
arms and scissored inches from her hair. Although they
would not permit her to accompany them to either of
the Sunday services they attended, she was included in
the daily prayers before breakfast, midmorning and
evening. But none of the surrender, begging, imploring
or praising on her knees took hold because, hard as she
fought, the Messalina part erupted anyway and the Presbyterians abandoned her without so much as a murmur
of fare well.

It was some time afterward while branch-sweeping
Sir's dirt floor, being careful to avoid the hen nesting in
the corner, lonely, angry and hurting, that she decided
to fortify herself by piecing together scraps of what her
mother had taught her before dying in agony. Relying
on memory and her own resources, she cobbled
together neglected rites, merged Europe medicine with
native, scripture with lore, and recalled or invented the
hidden meaning of things. Found, in other words, a way
to be in the world. There was no comfort or place for
her in the village; Sir was there and not there. Solitude
would have crushed her had she not fallen into hermit
skills and become one more thing that moved in the
natural world. She cawed with birds, chatted with

plants, spoke to squirrels, sang to the cow and opened her mouth to rain. The shame of having survived the destruction of her families shrank with her vow never to betray or abandon anyone she cherished. Memories of her village peopled by the dead turned slowly to ash and in their place a single image arose. Fire. How quick. How purposefully it ate what had been built, what had been life. Cleansing somehow and scandalous in beauty. Even before a simple hearth or encouraging a flame to boil water she felt a sweet twinge of agitation.

Waiting for the arrival of a wife, Sir was a hurricane of activity laboring to bring nature under his control. More than once when Lina brought his dinner to whatever field or woodlot he was working in, she found him, head thrown back, staring at the sky as if in wondering despair at the land's refusal to obey his will. Together they minded the fowl and starter stock; planted corn and vegetables. But it was she who taught him how to dry the fish they caught; to anticipate spawning and how to protect a crop from night creatures. Yet neither of them knew what to do about fourteen days of rain or fifty-five of none. They were helpless when black flies descended in scarves, disabling cattle, the horse, and forcing them to take refuge indoors. Lina didn't know too much herself, but she did know what a poor farmer he was. At least she was able to distinguish weed from seedling. Without patience, the lifeblood of farming, and reluctant to seek advice from villagers nearby, he was forever unprepared for violent, mocking changes in weather and for the fact that common predators neither knew nor cared to whom their prey belonged. He

ignored her warning of using alewives as fertilizer only
to see his plots of tender vegetables torn up by foragers
attracted by the smell. Nor would he plant squash
among the corn. Though he allowed that the vines kept
weeds away, he did not like the look of disorder. Yet he
was good with animals and building things.

It was an unrewarding life. Unless the weather was
dangerous, she nested with the chickens until, just
before the wife arrived, he threw up a cowshed in one
day. During all that time Lina must have said fifty words
other than "Yes, Sir." Solitude, regret and fury would
have broken her had she not erased those six years pre-
ceding the death of the world. The company of other
children, industrious mothers in beautiful jewelry, the
majestic plan of life: when to vacate, to harvest, to burn,
to hunt; ceremonies of death, birth and worship. She
sorted and stored what she dared to recall and eliminated the rest, an activity which shaped her inside and
out. By the time Mistress came, her self-invention was
almost perfected. Soon it was irresistible.

Lina placed magic pebbles under Mistress' pillow;
kept the room fresh with mint and forced angelica root
in her patient's festering mouth to pull bad spirits from
her body. She prepared the most powerful remedy she
knew: devil's bit, mugwort, Saint-John's-wort, maiden-
hair and periwinkle; boiled it, strained it and spooned it
between Mistress' teeth. She considered repeating some
of the prayers she learned among the Presbyterians, but
since none had saved Sir, she thought not. He went
quickly. Screaming at Mistress. Then whispering, begging to be taken to his third house. The big one, useless
now that there were no children or children's children to

live in it. No one to stand in awe at its size or to admire the sinister gate that the smithy took two months to make. Two copper snakes met at the top. When they parted it for Sir's last wish, Lina felt as though she were entering the world of the damned. But if the black-smith's work was a frivolous waste of a grown man's time, his presence was not. He brought one girl to wom-anhood and saved the life of another. Sorrow. Vixen-eyed Sorrow with black teeth and a head of never groomed woolly hair the color of a setting sun. Accepted, not bought, by Sir, she joined the household after Lina but before Florens and still had no memory of her past life except being dragged ashore by whales.

"Not whales," Mistress had said. "Certainly not. She was treading water in the North River in Mohawk country, half drowned, when two young sawyers trawled her in. They threw a blanket over her and brought their father to the riverbank where she lay. It's said she had been living alone on a foundered ship. They thought she was a boy."

Not then, not ever, had she spoken of how she got there or where she had been. The sawyer's wife named her Sorrow, for good reason, thought Lina, and follow-ing a winter of feeding the daft girl who kept wandering off getting lost, who knew nothing and worked less, a strange melancholy girl to whom her sons were paying very close attention, the sawyer's wife asked her husband to get quit of her. He obliged and offered her to the care of a customer he trusted to do her no harm. Sir. When Sorrow arrived, trailing Sir's horse, Mistress barely hid her annoyance but admitted the place could use the help. If Sir was bent on travel, two female farmers and a four-year-old daughter were not enough. Lina had been a tall fourteen-year-old when Sir bought her from the Presbyterians. He had searched the advertisements posted at the printer's in town. "A likely woman who has had small pox and measles. . . . A likely Negro about 9 years. . . . Girl or woman that is handy in the kitchen sensible, speaks good English, complexion between yellow and black. . . . Five years time of a white woman that understands Country work, with a child upwards of two years old. . . . Mulatto Fellow very much pitted with small pox, honest and sober. . . . White lad fit to serve. . . . Wanted a servant able to drive a carriage, white or black. . . . Sober and prudent woman who. . . . Likely wench, white, 29 years with child. . . . Healthy Deutsch woman for rent . . . stout healthy, healthy strong, strong healthy likely sober sober sober . . ." until he got to "Hardy female, Christianized and capable in all matters domestic available for exchange of goods or specie."

A bachelor expecting the arrival of a new wife, he required precisely that kind of female on his land. By then Lina's swollen eye had calmed and the lash cuts on her face, arms and legs had healed and were barely noticeable. The Presbyterians, recalling perhaps their own foresight in the name they had given her, never asked what had happened to her and there was no point in telling them. She had no standing in law, no surname and no one would take her word against a Europe. What they did was consult with the printer about the wording of an advertisement. "Hardy female . . ."

When the Europe wife stepped down from the cart, hostility between them was instant. The health and

beauty of a young female already in charge annoyed the
new wife; while the assumption of authority from the
awkward Europe girl infuriated Lina. Yet the animosity,
utterly useless in the wild, died in the womb. Even
before Lina midwifed Mistress' first child, neither one
could keep the coolness. The fraudulent competition
was worth nothing on land that demanding. Besides
they were company for each other and by and by dis-
covered something much more interesting than status.
Rebekka laughed out loud at her own mistakes; was
unembarrassed to ask for help. Lina slapped her own
forehead when she forgot the berries rotting in the
straw. They became friends. Not only because some-
body had to pull the wasp sting from the other's arm.
Not only because it took two to push the cow away from
the fence. Not only because one had to hold the head
while the other one tied the trotters. Mostly because
neither knew precisely what they were doing or how.
Together, by trial and error they learned: what kept the
foxes away; how and when to handle and spread
manure; the difference between lethal and edible and
the sweet taste of timothy grass; the features of measled
swine; what turned the baby's stool liquid and what
hardened it into pain. For her Mistress, farmwork was
more adventure than drudgery. Then again, thought
Lina, she had Sir who pleased her more and more and
soon a daughter, Patrician, both of whom dulled the
regret of the short-lived infants Lina delivered and
buried each subsequent year. By the time Sir brought
Sorrow home, the resident women were a united front
in dismay. To Mistress she was useless. To Lina she was
bad luck in the flesh. Red hair, black teeth, recurring

neck boils and a look in those over-lashed silver-gray eyes that raised Lina's nape hair.

She watched while Mistress trained Sorrow to sewing, the one task she liked and was good at, and said nothing when, to stop her roaming, he said, Sir made the girl sleep by the fireplace all seasons. A comfort Lina was suspicious of but did not envy even in bad weather. Her people had built sheltering cities for a thousand years and, except for the deathfeet of the Europes, might have built them for a thousand more. As it turned out the sachem had been dead wrong. The Europes neither fled nor died out. In fact, said the old women in charge of the children, he had apologized for his error in prophecy and admitted that however many collapsed from ignorance or disease more would always come. They would come with languages that sounded like dog bark; with a childish hunger for animal fur. They would forever fence land, ship whole trees to faraway countries, take any woman for quick pleasure, ruin soil, befoul sacred places and worship a dull, unimaginative god. They let their hogs browse the ocean shore turning it into dunes of sand where nothing green can ever grow again. Cut loose from the earth's soul, they insisted on purchase of its soil, and like all orphans they were insatiable. It was their destiny to chew up the world and spit out a horribleness that would destroy all primary peoples. Lina was not so sure. Based on the way Sir and Mistress tried to run their farm, she knew there were exceptions to the sachem's revised prophecy. They seemed mindful of a distinction between earth and property, fenced their cattle though their neighbors did

not, and although legal to do so, they were hesitant to
kill foraging swine. They hoped to live by tillage rather
than eat up the land with herds, measures that kept their
profit low. So while Lina trusted more or less Sir's and
Mistress' judgment, she did not trust their instincts.
Had they true insight they would never have kept Sorrow so close.

Hard company she was, needing constant attention,
as at this very daybreak when, out of necessity, she had
been trusted with the milking. Since being pregnant
hampered her on the stool, she mis-handled the udder,
and the cow, Sorrow reported, had kicked. Lina left the
sickroom to mind the heifer—talk to her first, hum a
little, then slowly cradle the tender teats with a palm of
cream. The spurts were sporadic, worthless, except for
the cow's relief, and after she had oiled her into comfort,
Lina rushed back into the house. No good could come
of leaving Mistress alone with Sorrow, and now that her
stomach was low with child, she was even less reliable.
In the best of times the girl dragged misery like a tail.
There was a man in Lina's village like that. His name she
had forgotten along with the rest of her language, but it
meant "trees fall behind him," suggesting his influence
on the surroundings. In Sorrow's presence eggs would
not allow themselves to be beaten into foam, nor did
butter lighten cake batter. Lina was sure the early deaths
of Mistress' sons could be placed at the feet of the natural curse that was Sorrow. After the death of the second
infant Lina felt obliged to inform her mistress of the
danger. They were making mincemeat to be ready for
Sir's return. The neats' feet which had been simmering

since morning were cool now. Their severed bones lay on the table, waiting for the addition of fat and gristle for boiling.

"Some people do evil purposefully," said Lina. "Others can't help the evil they make."

Mistress looked up. "What are you saying?"

"Your son, John Jacob. He died after Sorrow came."

"Stay, Lina. Don't feed old misery. My baby died of fever."

"But Patrician sickened too and did not—"

"I said stay. That he died in my arms is enough without adding savage nonsense." She went on describing all infants' frailty during teething, her voice stern as she chopped the meat then stirred in raisins, apple slices, ginger, sugar and salt. Lina pushed a large jar closer and the two of them spooned the mixture into it. Then Lina filled the jar to the top with brandy and sealed it. Four weeks or more outside and it would be ready for a crust at Christmas. Meantime, Mistress dropped the brain and heart of a calf into a pot of boiling seasoned water. Such a supper, fried in butter and garnished with egg slices, would be a treat.

Now, more than unreliable, more than wandering off to talk to grass and grapevines, Sorrow was pregnant and soon there would be another virgin birth and, perhaps, unfortunately, this one would not die. But if Mistress died, what then? To whom could they turn? Although the Baptists once freely helped Sir build the second house, the outhouses, and happily joined him in felling white pine for the post fence, a cooling had risen between them and his family. Partly because Mistress hated them for shutting her children out of heaven, but also, thought Lina, because Sorrow's lurking frightened them. Years past, the Baptists might bring a brace of salmon or offer a no-longer-needed cradle for Mistress' baby. And the deacon could be counted on for baskets of strawberries and blue, all manner of nuts and once a whole haunch of venison. Now, of course, nobody, Baptist or any other, would come to a poxed house. Neither Willard nor Scully came, which should not have disappointed her, but did. Both were Europes, after all. Willard was getting on in years and was still working off his passage. The original seven years stretched to twenty-some, he said, and he had long ago forgotten most of the mischief that kept extending his bondage. The ones he remembered with a smile involved rum; the others were attempts to run away. Scully, young, fine-boned, with light scars tracing his back, had plans. He was finishing his mother's contract. True, he didn't know how long it would take but, he boasted, unlike Willard's or Lina's, his enslavement would end before death. He was the son of a woman sent off to the colonies for "lewdness and disobedience," neither of which according to him was quelled. Her death transferred her contract to her son. Then a man claiming to be Scully's father settled the balance owed and recuperated certain expenses by leasing the boy to his current master for a span of time soon to end, although Scully was not privy to exactly when. There was a legal paper, he had told Lina, that said it. Lina guessed he had not seen it and could not cipher it if he had. All he knew for certain was that the freedom fee would be generous enough to purchase a horse or set him up in a trade. What trade, wondered Lina. If that glorious day of freedom fees did not arrive soon, he too, she thought, will run away, and maybe have the good fortune denied Willard. Cleverer than the older man, and sober, he might succeed. Still, she doubted it; thought his dreams of selling his labor were only that. She knew he did not object to lying with Willard when sleep was not the point. No wonder Sir, without kin or sons to count on, had no males on his property. It made good sense, except when it didn't. As now with two lamenting women, one confined to bed, the other heavily pregnant; a love-broken girl on the loose and herself unsure of everything including moonrise.

Don't die, Miss. Don't. Herself, Sorrow, a newborn and maybe Florens—three unmastered women and an infant out here, alone, belonging to no one, became wild game for anyone. None of them could inherit; none was attached to a church or recorded in its books. Female and illegal, they would be interlopers, squatters, if they stayed on after Mistress died, subject to purchase, hire, assault, abduction, exile. The farm could be claimed by or auctioned off to the Baptists. Lina had relished her place in this small, tight family, but now saw its folly. Sir and Mistress believed they could have honest free-thinking lives, yet without heirs, all their work meant less than a swallow's nest. Their drift away from others produced a selfish privacy and they had lost the refuge and the consolation of a clan. Baptists, Presbyterians, tribe, army, family, some encircling outside thing was needed. Pride, she thought. Pride alone made them think that they needed only themselves, could shape life that way, like Adam and Eve, like gods from

nowhere beholden to nothing except their own crea-
tions. She should have warned them, but her devotion
cautioned against impertinence. As long as Sir was alive
it was easy to veil the truth: that they were not a
family—not even a like-minded group. They were
orphans, each and all.

Lina gazed through the wavy pane of the tiny window where a flirtatious sun poured soft yellow light
toward the foot of Mistress' bed. Beyond on the far side
of the trail stood a forest of beech. As was often the case,
she spoke to them.

"You and I, this land is our home," she whispered,
"but unlike you I am exile here."

Lina's mistress is mumbling now, telling Lina or herself some tale, some matter of grave importance as the
dart of her eyes showed. What was so vital, Lina wondered, that she uses an unworkable tongue in a mouth
lined with sores? Her wrapped hands lift and wave. Lina
turns to look where the eyes focus. A trunk where Mistress kept pretty things, treasured unused gifts from Sir.
A lace collar, a hat no decent woman would be seen in,
its peacock feather already broken in the press. On top
of a few lengths of silk lay a small mirror set in an elaborate frame, its silver tarnished to soot.

"Gi' me," said Mistress.

Lina picked up the mirror thinking, No, please.
Don't look. Never seek out your own face even when
well, lest the reflection drink your soul.

"Hur-ee," moaned Mistress, her tone pleading like a
child's.

Helpless to disobey, Lina brought it to the lady. She

placed it between the mittened hands, certain now that her mistress will die. And the certainty was a kind of death for herself as well, since her own life, everything, depended on Mistress' survival, which depended on Florens' success.

Lina had fallen in love with her right away, as soon as she saw her shivering in the snow. A frightened, long-necked child who did not speak for weeks but when she did her light, singsong voice was lovely to hear. Some how, some way, the child assuaged the tiny yet eternal yearning for the home Lina once knew where everyone had anything and no one had everything. Perhaps her own barrenness sharpened her devotion. In any case, she wanted to protect her, keep her away from the corruption so natural to someone like Sorrow, and, most recently, she was determined to be the wall between Florens and the blacksmith. Since his coming, there was an appetite in the girl that Lina recognized as once her own. A bleating desire beyond sense, without conscience. The young body speaking in its only language its sole reason for life on earth. When he arrived—too shiny, way too tall, both arrogant and skilled—Lina alone saw the peril, but there was no one to complain to. Mistress was silly with happiness because her husband was home and Sir behaved as though the blacksmith was his brother. Lina had seen them bending their heads over lines drawn in dirt. Another time she saw Sir slice a green apple, his left boot raised on a rock, his mouth working along with his hands; the smithy nodding, looking intently at his employer. Then Sir, as nonchalantly as you please, tipped a slice of apple on his knife

and offered it to the blacksmith who, just as nonchalantly, took it and put it in his mouth. So Lina knew she
was the only one alert to the breakdown stealing toward
them. The only one who foresaw the disruption, the
shattering a free black man would cause. He had already
ruined Florens, since she refused to see that she han-
kered after a man that had not troubled to tell her goodbye. When Lina tried to enlighten her, saying, "You are
one leaf on his tree," Florens shook her head, closed her
eyes and replied, "No. I am his tree." A sea change that
Lina could only hope was not final.

Florens had been a quiet, timid version of herself at
the time of her own displacement. Before destruction.
Before sin. Before men. Lina had hovered over Patrician,
competing with Mistress for the little girl's affection, but
this one, coming on the heels of Patrician's death, could
be, would be, her own. And she would be the opposite
of incorrigible Sorrow. Already Florens could read,
write. Already she did not have to be told repeatedly
how to complete a chore. Not only was she consistently
trustworthy, she was deeply grateful for every shred of
affection, any pat on the head, any smile of approval.
They had memorable nights, lying together, when Florens listened in rigid delight to Lina's stories. Stories of
wicked men who chopped off the heads of devoted
wives; of cardinals who carried the souls of good children to a place where time itself was a baby. Especially
called for were stories of mothers fighting to save their
children from wolves and natural disasters. Close to
heartbreak, Lina recalled a favorite and the whispered
conversation that always followed it.

One day, ran the story, an eagle laid her eggs in a nest far above and far beyond the snakes and paws that hunted them. Her eyes are midnight black and shiny as she watches over them. At the tremble of a leaf, the scent of any other life, her frown deepens, her head jerks and her feathers quietly lift. Her talons are sharpened on rock; her beak is like the scythe of a war god. She is fierce, protecting her borning young. But one thing she cannot defend against: the evil thoughts of man. One day a traveler climbs a mountain nearby. He stands at its summit admiring all he sees below him. The turquoise lake, the eternal hemlocks, the starlings sailing into clouds cut by rainbow. The traveler laughs at the beauty saying, "This is perfect. This is mine." And the word swells, booming like thunder into valleys, over acres of primrose and mallow. Creatures come out of caves wondering what it means. Mine. Mine. Mine. The shells of the eagle's eggs quiver and one even cracks. The eagle swivels her head to find the source of the strange, meaningless thunder, the incomprehensible sound. Spotting the traveler, she swoops down to claw away his laugh and his unnatural sound. But the traveler, under attack, raises his stick and strikes her wing with all his strength. Screaming she falls and falls. Over the turquoise lake, beyond the eternal hemlocks, down through the clouds cut by rainbow. Screaming, screaming she is carried away by wind instead of wing.

Then Florens would whisper, "Where is she now?"

"Still falling," Lina would answer, "she is falling forever."

Florens barely breathes. "And the eggs?" she asks.

"They hatch alone," says Lina.

"Do they live?" Florens' whispering is urgent.

"We have," says Lina.

Florens would sigh then, her head on Lina's shoulder and when sleep came the little girl's smile lingered. Mother hunger—to be one or have one—both of them were reeling from that longing which, Lina knew, remained alive, traveling the bone. As Florens grew, she learned quickly, was eager to know more and would have been the perfect one to find the blacksmith if only she had not been crippled with worship of him.

When Mistress insisted on unhinging herself by staring at her face in the mirror, Lina closed her eyes against that reckless solicitation of bad luck and left the room. A heap of chores beckoned and, as always, Sorrow was not to be found. Pregnant or not, she could at least have mucked out the stalls. Lina entered the cowshed and glanced at the broken sleigh where, in cold weather, she and Florens slept. At the sight of cobwebs strung from blade to bed, Lina sighed, then caught her breath. Florens' shoes, the rabbit skin ones she had made for her ten years ago, lay under the sleigh—lonely, empty like two patient coffins. Shaken, she left the shed and stood still at the door. Where to go? She couldn't endure the self-pity that drove Mistress to tempt harmful spirits, so she decided to look for Sorrow down by the river where she often went to talk to her dead baby.

The river gleamed under a sun departing slowly like a bride reluctant to leave the marriage feast. No Sorrow anywhere, but Lina caught the delicious smell of fire and followed it. Cautiously she moved toward the odor of smoke. Soon she heard voices, several, carefully, deliberately low. Creeping a hundred yards or so toward the sound she saw figures lit by a small fire dug deep in the ground. A boy and several adults camped in winter-green beneath two hawthorns. One man was asleep, another whittling. Three women, two of whom were Europes, seemed to be clearing away signs of a meal, nutshells, corn husks, and repacking other items. Unarmed, probably peaceful, thought Lina as she came closer. As soon as she let herself be seen, they scrambled up—all but the sleeping man. Lina recognized them from the wagon Florens had boarded. Her heart seized. What happened?

"Evening," said the man.

"Evening," replied Lina.

"Is this your land, Ma'am?" he asked.

"No. But you are welcome here."

"Well, thank you. We won't tarry." He relaxed as did the others.

"I remember you," said Lina. "From the wagon. To Hartkill."

There was a long silence as they considered an answer.

Lina went on, "There was a maid with you. I put her aboard."

"There was," said the man.

"What happened to her?"

The women shook their heads and shrugged. "She left the wagon," said one.

Lina placed her hand beneath her throat. "She got off? Why?"

"Couldn't say. She went into the woods I believe."

"By herself?"

"We offered her to join us. She chose not to. Seemed in a hurry."

"Where? Where did she get off?"

"Same as us. The tavern."

"I see," said Lina. She didn't, but thought it best not to press. "Shall I bring you anything? The farm is nearby."

"Appreciate it, but no thank you. We journey at night."

The sleeping man was awake now, looking carefully at Lina while the other one seemed intent on the river. When they had finished collecting their few supplies, one of the Europe women said to the others,

"We'd better be down there. He won't wait."

They agreed without saying so, and started toward the river.

"Fare well," said Lina.

"Goodbye. Bless you."

Then the first man turned back. "You never saw us, did you, Ma'am?"

"No. I never did."

"Much obliged," he said and tipped his hat.

Walking back toward the house, taking pains to avoid even looking at the new one, Lina was relieved that so far nothing bad had happened to Florens, and more frightened than ever that something would. The runaways had one purpose; Florens had another. Instead of entering the house, Lina wandered to the road, looked both ways, then lifted her head to smell oncoming weather. Spring, as usual, was skittish. Five days ago the rain she smelled coming was longer and harder than it had been in some time; a downpour she thought hastened Sir's death. Then a day of hot, bright sun that freshened and tinted trees into pale green mist. The sudden snow that followed surprised and alarmed her since Florens would be traveling through it. Now, knowing Florens had pressed on, she tried to learn what the sky, the breezes, had in store. Calm, she decided; spring was settling itself into growing season. Reassured, she went back into the sickroom where she heard Mistress mumbling. More self-pity? No, not an apology to her own face this time. Now, amazingly, she was praying. For what, to what, Lina did not know. She was both startled and embarrassed, since she had always thought Mistress polite to the Christian god, but indifferent, if not hostile, to religion. Well, Lina mused, deathbreath was a prime creator, a great changer of minds and collector of hearts. Any decision made while inhaling it was as unreliable as it was fierce. Reason in moments of crisis was rare. Yet, what about Florens? Look what she did when things changed abruptly: chose to go her own route once the others had crept away. Correctly. Bravely. But could she manage? Alone? She had Sir's boots, the letter, food and a desperate need to see the blacksmith. But will she return, with him, after him, without him, or not at all?

Night is thick no stars anyplace but sudden the moon moves. The chafe of needles is too much hurt and there is no resting there at all. I get down and look for a better place. By moonlight I am happy to find a hollow log, but it is wavy with ants. I break off twigs and small branches from a young fir, pile them and crawl under. The needle prick is smaller and there is no danger of falling. The ground is damp, chill. Night voles come close, sniff me then dart away. I am watchful for snakes that ease down trees and over ground, although Lina says they do not prefer to bite us or swallow us whole. I lie still and try not to think of water. Thinking instead of another night, another place of wet ground. But it is summer then and the damp is from dew not snow. You are telling me about the making of iron things. How happy you are to find easy ore so close to the surface of

the earth. The glory of shaping metal. Your father doing
it and his father before him back and back for a thousand years. With furnaces from termite mounds. And
you know the ancestors approve when two owls appear
at the very instant you say their names so you understand they are showing themselves to bless you. See, you
say, see how they swivel their heads. They approve you
also, you tell me. Do they bless me too, I ask. Wait,
you say. Wait and see. I think they do, because I am
coming now. I am coming to you.

Lina says there are some spirits who look after warriors and hunters and there are others who guard virgins
and mothers. I am none of those. Reverend Father says
communion is the best hope, prayer the next. There is
no communion hereabouts and I feel shame to speak to
the Virgin when all I am asking for is not to her liking. I
think Mistress has nothing to say on the matter. She
avoids the Baptists and the village women who go to the
meetinghouse. They annoy her as when we three, Mistress, Sorrow and me, go to sell two calves. They are
trotting behind us on rope to the cart we ride in. We
wait while Mistress does the selling talk. Sorrow jumps
down and goes behind the trader's post where a village
woman slaps her face many times and screams at her.
When Mistress discovers what is happening, both her
face and the village woman's burn in anger. Sorrow is
relieving herself in the yard without care for the eyes of
others. The argue is done and Mistress drives us away.
After a while she pulls the horse to a stop. She turns to
Sorrow and slaps her face more, saying Fool. I am shock.
Mistress never strikes us. Sorrow does not cry or answer.

I think Mistress says other words to her, softer ones, but I am only seeing how her eyes go. Their look is close to the way of the women who stare at Lina and me as we wait for the Ney brothers. Neither look scares, but it is a hurting thing. But I know Mistress has a sweeter heart. On a winter day when I am still small Lina asks her if she can give me the dead daughter's shoes. They are black with six buttons each. Mistress agrees but when she sees me in them she sudden sits down in the snow and cries. Sir comes and picks her up in his arms and carries her into the house.

I never cry. Even when the woman steals my cloak and shoes and I am freezing on the boat no tears come.

These thoughts are sad in me, so I make me think of you instead. How you say your work in the world is strong and beautiful. I think you are also. No holy spirits are my need. No communion or prayer. You are my protection. Only you. You can be it because you say you are a free man from New Amsterdam and always are that. Not like Will or Scully but like Sir. I don't know the feeling of or what it means, free and not free. But I have a memory. When Sir's gate is done and you are away so long, I walk sometimes to search you. Behind the new house, the rise, over the hill beyond. I see a path between rows of elm trees and enter it. Underfoot is weed and soil. In a while the path turns away from the elms and to my right is land dropping away in rocks. To my left is a hill. High, very high. Climbing over it all, up up, are scarlet flowers I never see before. Everywhere choking their own leaves. The scent is sweet. I put my hand in to gather a few blossoms. I hear something behind me and turn to see a stag moving up the rock side. He is great. And grand. Standing there between the beckoning wall of perfume and the stag I wonder what else the world may show me. It is as though I am loose to do what I choose, the stag, the wall of flowers. I am a little scare of this looseness. Is that how free feels? I don't like it. I don't want to be free of you because I am live only with you. When I choose and say good morning, the stag bounds away.

Now I am thinking of another thing. Another animal that shapes choice. Sir bathes every May. We pour buckets of hot water into the washtub and gather wintergreen to sprinkle in. He sits awhile. His knees poke up, his hair is flat and wet over the edge. Soon Mistress is there with first a rock of soap, then a short broom. After he is rosy with scrubbing he stands. She wraps a cloth around to dry him. Later she steps in and splashes herself. He does not scrub her. He is in the house to dress himself. A moose moves through the trees at the edge of the clearing. We all, Mistress, Lina and me, see him. He stands alone looking. Mistress crosses her wrists over her breasts. Her eyes are big and stare. Her face loses its blood. Lina shouts and throws a stone. The moose turns slowly and walks away. Like a chieftain. Still Mistress trembles as though a wicked thing has come. I am thinking how small she looks. It is only a moose who has no interest in her. Or anyone. Mistress does not shout or keep to her splashing. She will not risk to choose. Sir steps out. Mistress stands up and rushes to him. Her naked skin is aslide with wintergreen. Lina and I look at each other. What is she fearing, I ask.

Nothing, says Lina. Why then does she run to Sir? Because she can, Lina answers. Sudden a sheet of sparrows fall from the sky and settle in the trees. So many the trees seem to sprout birds, not leaves at all. Lina points. We never shape the world she says. The world shapes us. Sudden and silent the sparrows are gone. I am not understanding Lina. You are my shaper and my world as well. It is done. No need to choose.

How long will it take will she get lost will he be there will he come will some vagrant rape her? She needed shoes, proper shoes, to replace the dirty scraps that covered her feet, and it was only when Lina made her some did she say a word.

Rebekka's thoughts bled into one another, confusing events and time but not people. The need to swallow, the pain of doing so, the unbearable urge to tear her skin from the bones underneath stopped only when she was unconscious—not asleep, because as far as the dreams were concerned it was the same as being awake.

"I shat among strangers for six weeks to get to this land."

She has told this to Lina over and over. Lina being the only one left whose understanding she trusted and whose judgment she valued. Even now, in the deep blue of a spring night, with less sleep than her Mistress, Lina was whispering and shaking a feathered stick around the bed.

"Among strangers," said Rebekka. "There was no other way packed like cod between decks."

She fixed her eyes on Lina who had put away her wand and now knelt by the bed.

"I know you," said Rebekka, and thought she was smiling although she was not sure. Other familiar faces sometimes hovered, then went away: her daughter; the sailor who helped carry her boxes and tighten their straps; a man on the gallows. No. This face was real. She recognized the dark anxious eyes, the tawny skin. How could she not know the single friend she had? To confirm to herself that moment of clarity, she said, "Lina. Remember, do you? We didn't have a fireplace. It was cold. So cold. I thought she was a mute or deaf, you know. Blood is sticky. It never goes away however much . . ." Her voice was intense, confidential as though revealing a secret. Then silence as she fell somewhere between fever and memory.

There was nothing in the world to prepare her for a life of water, on water, about water; sickened by it and desperate for it. Mesmerized and bored by the look of it, especially at midday when the women were allowed another hour on deck. Then she talked to the sea. "Stay still, don't hurtle me. No. Move, move, excite me. Trust me, I will keep your secrets: that the smell of you is like fresh monthly blood; that you own the globe and land is afterthought to entertain you; that the world beneath you is both graveyard and heaven."

Immediately upon landing Rebekka's sheer good fortune in a husband stunned her. Already sixteen, she knew her father would have shipped her off to anyone who would book her passage and relieve him of feeding her. A waterman, he was privy to all sorts of news from colleagues, and when a crewman passed along an inquiry from a first mate—a search for a healthy, chaste wife willing to travel abroad—he was quick to offer his eldest girl. The stubborn one, the one with too many questions and a rebellious mouth. Rebekka's mother objected to the "sale"—she called it that because the prospective groom had stressed "reimbursement" for clothing, expenses and a few supplies—not for love or need of her daughter, but because the husband-to-be was a heathen living among savages. Religion, as Rebekka experienced it from her mother, was a flame fueled by a wondrous hatred. Her parents treated each other and their children with glazed indifference and saved their fire for religious matters. Any drop of generosity to a stranger threatened to douse the blaze. Rebekka's understanding of God was faint, except as a larger kind of king, but she quieted the shame of insufficient devotion by assuming that He could be no grander nor better than the imagination of the believer. Shallow believers preferred a shallow god. The timid enjoyed a rampaging avenging god. In spite of her father's eagerness, her mother warned her that savages or nonconformists would slaughter her as soon as she landed, so when Rebekka found Lina already there, waiting outside the one-room cottage her new husband had built for them, she bolted the door at night and

would not let the raven-haired girl with impossible skin
sleep anywhere near. Fourteen or so, stone-faced she
was, and it took a while for trust between them. Perhaps
because both were alone without family, or because both
had to please one man, or because both were hopelessly
ignorant of how to run a farm, they became what was
for each a companion. A pair, anyway, the result of the
mute alliance that comes of sharing tasks. Then, when
the first infant was born, Lina handled it so tenderly,
with such knowing, Rebekka was ashamed of her early
fears and pretended she'd never had them. Now, lying
in bed, her hands wrapped and bound against self-
mutilation, her lips drawn back from her teeth, she
turned her fate over to others and became prey to scenes
of past disorder. The first hangings she saw in the square
amid a happy crowd attending. She was probably two
years old, and the death faces would have frightened
her if the crowd had not mocked and enjoyed them
so. With the rest of her family and most of their
neighbors, she was present at a drawing and quartering
and, although she was too young to remember the
details, her nightmares were made permanently vivid by
years of retelling and redescribing by her parents. She
did not know what a Fifth Monarchist was, then or now,
but it was clear in her household that execution was a
festivity as exciting as a king's parade.

Brawls, knifings and kidnaps were so common in the
city of her birth that the warnings of slaughter in a new,
unseen world were like threats of bad weather. The very
year she stepped off the ship a mighty settlers-versus-
natives war two hundred miles away was over before she

heard of it. The intermittent skirmishes of men against men, arrows against powder, fire against hatchet that she heard of could not match the gore of what she had seen since childhood. The pile of frisky, still living entrails held before the felon's eyes then thrown into a bucket and tossed into the Thames; fingers trembling for a lost torso; the hair of a woman guilty of mayhem bright with flame. Compared to that, death by shipwreck or toma-hawk paled. She did not know what other settler fami-lies nearby once knew of routine dismemberment, but she did not share their dread when, three months after the incident, news came of a pitched battle, a kidnap or a peace gone awry. The squabbles between local tribes or militia peppering parts of the region seemed a distant, manageable backdrop in a land of such space and per-fume. The absence of city and shipboard stench rocked her into a kind of drunkenness that it took years to sober up from and take sweet air for granted. Rain itself became a brand-new thing: clean, sootless water falling from the sky. She clasped her hands under her chin gaz-ing at trees taller than a cathedral, wood for warmth so plentiful it made her laugh, then weep, for her brothers and the children freezing in the city she had left behind. She had never seen birds like these, or tasted fresh water that ran over visible white stones. There was adventure in learning to cook game she'd never heard of and acquiring a taste for roast swan. Well, yes, there were monstrous storms here with snow piled higher than the sill of a shutter. And summer insects swarmed with song louder than chiming steeple bells. Yet the thought of what her life would have been had she stayed crushed into those reeking streets, spat on by lords and prostitutes, curtseying, curtseying, curtseying, still repelled her. Here she answered to her husband alone and paid polite attendance (time and weather permitting) to the only meetinghouse in the area. Anabaptists who were not the Satanists her parents called them, as they did all Separatists, but sweet, generous people for all their confounding views. Views that got them and the horrible Quakers beaten bloody in their own meetinghouse back home. Rebekka had no bone-deep hostility. Even the king had pardoned a dozen of them on their way to the gallows. She still remembered her parents' disappointment when the festivities were canceled and their fury at an easily swayed monarch. Her discomfort in a garret full of constant argument, bursts of enraged envy and sullen disapproval of anyone not like them made her impatient for some kind of escape. Any kind.

There had been an early rescue, however, and the possibility of better things in Church School where she was chosen as one of four to be trained for domestic service. But the one place that agreed to take her turned out to require running from the master and hiding behind doors. She lasted four days. After that no one offered her another place. Then came the bigger rescue when her father got notice of a man looking for a strong wife rather than a dowry. Between the warning of immediate slaughter and the promise of married bliss, she believed in neither. Yet without money or the inclination to peddle goods, open a stall or be apprenticed in exchange for food and shelter, with even nunneries for the upper class banned, her prospects were servant,

prostitute, wife, and although horrible stories were told
about each of those careers, the last one seemed safest.
The one where she might have children and therefore be
guaranteed some affection. As with any future available
to her, it depended on the character of the man in
charge. Hence marriage to an unknown husband in a
far-off land had distinct advantages: separation from a
mother who had barely escaped the ducking pond; from
male siblings who worked days and nights with her
father and learned from him their dismissive attitude
toward the sister who had helped rear them; but especially escape from the leers and rude hands of any man,
drunken or sober, she might walk by. America. Whatever the danger, how could it possibly be worse?

Early on when she settled on Jacob's land, she visited
the local church some seven miles away and met a few
vaguely suspicious villagers. They had removed themselves from a larger sect in order to practice a purer form
of their Separatist religion, one truer and more acceptable to God. Among them she was deliberately soft-
spoken. In their meetinghouse she was accommodating
and when they explained their beliefs she did not roll
her eyes. It was when they refused to baptize her firstborn, her exquisite daughter, that Rebekka turned away.
Weak as her faith was, there was no excuse for not protecting the soul of an infant from eternal perdition.

More and more it was in Lina's company that she let
the misery seep out.

"I chastised her for a torn shift, Lina, and the next
thing I know she is lying in the snow. Her little head
cracked like an egg."

It would have embarrassed her to mention personal sorrow in prayer; to be other than stalwart in grief; to let God know she was less than thankful for His watch. But she had delivered four healthy babies, watched three surrender at a different age to one or another illness, and then watched Patrician, her firstborn, who reached the age of five and provided a happiness Rebekka could not believe, lie in her arms for two days before dying from a broken crown. And then to bury her twice. First in a fur-sheltered coffin because the ground could not accept the little box Jacob built, so they had to leave her to freeze in it and, second, in late spring when they could place her among her brothers with the Anabaptists attending. Weak, pustulate, with not even a full day to mourn Jacob, her grief was fresh cut, like hay in famine. Her own death was what she should be concentrating on. She could hear its hooves clacking on the roof, could see the cloaked figure on horseback. But whenever the immediate torment subsided, her thoughts left Jacob and traveled to Patrician's matted hair, the hard, dark lump of soap she used to clean it, the rinses over and over to free every honey-brown strand from the awful blood darkening, like her mind, to black. Rebekka never looked at the coffin waiting under pelts for thaw. But when finally the earth softened, when Jacob could get traction with the spade and they let the coffin down, she sat on the ground holding on to her elbows, oblivious of the damp, and gazed at every clod and clump that fell. She stayed there all day and through the night. No one, not Jacob, Sorrow or Lina, could get her up. And not the Pastor either, since he and his flock had been the ones whose beliefs stripped her children of redemption. She growled when they touched her; threw the blanket from her shoulders. They left her alone then, shaking their heads, muttering prayers for her forgiveness. At dawn in a light snowfall Lina came and arranged jewelry and food on the grave, along with scented leaves, telling her that the boys and Patrician were stars now, or something equally lovely: yellow and green birds, playful foxes or the rose-tinted clouds collecting at the edge of the sky. Pagan stuff, true, but more satisfying than the I-accept-and-will-see-you-at-Judgment-Day prayers Rebekka had been taught and heard repeated by the Baptist congregation. There had been a summer day once when she sat in front of the house sewing and talking profanely while Lina stirred linen boiling in a kettle at her side.

I don't think God knows who we are. I think He would like us, if He knew us, but I don't think He knows about us.

But He made us, Miss. No?

He did. But he made the tails of peacocks too. That must have been harder.

Oh, but, Miss, we sing and talk. Peacocks do not.

We need to. Peacocks don't. What else do we have?

Thoughts. Hands to make things.

All well and good. But that's our business. Not God's. He's doing something else in the world. We are not on His mind.

What is He doing then, if not watching over us?

Lord knows.

And they sputtered with laughter, like little girls hiding behind the stable loving the danger of their talk. She could not decide if Patrician's accident by a cloven hoof was rebuke or proof of the pudding.

Now here in bed, her deft, industrious hands wrapped in cloth lest she claw herself bloody, she could not tell if she was speaking aloud or simply thinking.

"I shat in a tub . . . strangers . . ."

Sometimes they circled her bed, these strangers who were not, who had become the kind of family sea journeys create. Delirium or Lina's medicine, she supposed. But they came and offered her advice, gossiped, laughed or simply stared at her with pity.

There were seven other women assigned to steerage on the *Angelus*. Waiting to board, their backs turned against the breeze that cut from sea to port, they shivered among boxes, bailiffs, upper-deck passengers, carts, horses, guards, satchels and weeping children. Finally, when lower-deck passengers were called to board, and their name, home county and occupation were recorded, four or five women said they were servants. Rebekka learned otherwise soon enough, soon as they were separated from males and the better-classed women and led to a dark space below next to the animal stalls. Light and weather streamed from a hatch; a tub for waste sat beside a keg of cider; a basket and a rope where food could be let down and the basket retrieved. Anyone taller than five feet hunched and lowered her head to move around. Crawling was easier once, like street vagrants, they partitioned off their personal space. The range of baggage, clothes, speech and attitude spoke clearly of who they were long before their confessions. One, Anne, had been sent away in disgrace by her family. Two, Judith and Lydia, were prostitutes ordered to choose between prison or exile. Lydia was accompanied by her daughter, Patty, a ten-year-old thief. Elizabeth was the daughter, or so she said, of an important Company agent. Another, Abigail, was quickly transferred to the captain's cabin and one other, Dorothea, was a cutpurse whose sentence was the same as the prostitutes'. Rebekka alone, her passage prepaid, was to be married. The rest were being met by relatives or craftsmen who would pay their passage—except the cutpurse and the whores whose costs and keep were to be borne by years and years of unpaid labor. Only Rebekka was none of these. It was later, huddled 'tween decks and walls made of trunks, boxes, blankets hanging from hammocks, that Rebekka learned more about them. The prepubescent girl thief-in-training had the singing voice of an angel. The agent's "daughter" was born in France. By the time they were fourteen the two mature prostitutes had been turned out of their family homes for lewd behavior. And the cutpurse was the niece of another one who taught and refined her skills. Together they lightened the journey; made it less hideous than it surely would have been without them. Their alehouse wit, their know-how laced with their low expectations of others and high levels of self-approval, their quick laughter, amused and encouraged Rebekka. If she had feared her own female vulnerability, traveling alone to a foreign country to wed a stranger, these women corrected her misgivings. If ever night moths fluttered in her chest at the recollection of her mother's predictions, the company of these exiled, thrown-away women eliminated them. Dorothea, with whom she became most friendly, was especially helpful. With exaggerated sighs and mild curses they sorted their possessions and appropriated territory no bigger than a doorstep. When under direct questioning, Rebekka admitted she was to be wed and, yes, for the first time, Dorothea laughed and announced the find to everyone in earshot. "A virgin! Judy, do you hear? An unripe cunt among us."

"Well, two aboard, then. Patty is another." Judith winked and smiled at the little girl. "Don't trade it cheap."

"She's ten!" said Lydia. "What shape of mother do you take me for?"

"In two years we'll answer."

The laughter was loud among the three, until Anne said, "Enough, please! Rudeness offends me."

"Rude words but not rude behavior?" asked Judith.

"That, too," she replied.

They were settled now and eager to test their neighbors. Dorothea removed a shoe and wiggled her toes through the stocking's hole. Then, tugging carefully, she folded the frayed wool under her toes. Replacing the shoe, she smiled at Anne.

"Is behavior the reason your family put you to sea?" Dorothea opened her eyes wide, batting her eyelashes at Anne in mock innocence.

"I'm visiting my uncle and aunt." If the light coming from the open hatch above had been stronger, they might have seen the crimson of her cheeks.

"And bringing them a present, I reckon." Lydia giggled.

"Coo, coo. Coo, coo." Dorothea cradled her arms.

"Cows!" snarled Anne.

More laughter loud enough to agitate the animals behind the planks that separated the women from the stock. A crewman, perhaps on orders, stood above them and closed the hatch.

"Bastard!" someone shouted as they were plunged into darkness. Dorothea and Lydia, crawling around, managed to find the sole lamp available. Once lit, the dollop of light pulled them close.

"Where is Miss Abigail?" asked Patty. She had taken a liking to her port side, hours before they set sail.

"Captain's pick," said her mother.

"Lucky whore," Dorothea murmured.

"Bite your tongue. You haven't seen him."

"No, but I can surmise his table." Dorothea sighed. "Berries, wine, mutton, pasties . . ."

"Tormentor. Leave off. Steady. Maybe the slut will send us some. He won't let her out of his sight. Pig . . ."

"Milk straight from the udder, no dirt or flies on top, stamped butter . . ."

"Leave off!"

"I have some cheese," said Rebekka. Surprised how like a child's her voice sounded, she coughed. "And biscuits."

They turned to her and a voice chimed, "Aw, lovely. Let's have tea."

The oil lamp sputtered, threatening to throw them back into a darkness only travelers in steerage can know. Rocking forever sideways, trying not to vomit before reaching the tub, safer on knees than feet—all was just bearable if there were even a handspan of light.

The women scooted toward Rebekka and suddenly,

without urging, began to imitate what they thought were the manners of queens. Judith spread her shawl on the lid of a box. Elizabeth retrieved from her trunk a kettle and a set of spoons. Cups were varied—pewter, tin, clay. Lydia heated water in the kettle over the lamp, protecting the flame with her palm. It did not surprise them that no one had any tea, but both Judith and Dorothea had rum hidden in their sacks. With the care of a butler, they poured it into the tepid water. Rebekka set the cheese in the middle of the shawl and surrounded it with biscuits. Anne offered grace. Breathing quietly, they sipped warm, spirited water and munched stale biscuits, daintily brushing away the flakes. Patty sat between her mother's knees, and Lydia tipped her cup with one hand and smoothed her daughter's hair with the other. Rebekka recalled how each of them, including the ten-year-old, lifted her little finger and angled it out. Remembered also how ocean slap exaggerated the silence. Perhaps they were blotting out, as she was, what they fled and what might await them. Wretched as was the space they crouched in, it was nevertheless blank where a past did not haunt nor a future beckon. Women of and for men, in those few moments they were neither. And when finally the lamp died, swaddling them in black, for a long time, oblivious to the footsteps above them, or the lowing behind them, they did not stir. For them, unable to see the sky, time became simply the running sea, unmarked, eternal and of no matter.

Upon landing they made no pretense of meeting again. They knew they never would, so their parting was brisk, unsentimental as each gathered her baggage and scanned the crowd for her future. It was true; they never met again, except for those bedside visits Rebekka conjured up.

He was bigger than she imagined. All the men she had known were small, hardened but small. Mr. Vaark (it took some time before she could say Jacob) picked up both of her boxes after touching her face and smiling.

"You took off your hat and smiled. Smiled and smiled." Rebekka thought she was answering the grin of her new husband, but her parched lips barely moved as she entered the scene of their first meeting. She had the impression, then, that this was what his whole life had been about: meeting her at long last, so obvious was his relief and satisfaction. Following him, feeling the disabling resilience of land after weeks at sea, she tripped on the wooden walk and tore the hem of her frock. He did not turn around so she grabbed a fistful of skirt, clutched her bedding under her arm and trotted along to the wagon, refusing the hand he offered to help her mount. It was seal and deal. He would offer her no pampering. She would not accept it if he did. A perfect equation for the work that lay ahead.

"Marriages performed within," read the sign next to the coffeehouse door, and underneath in small letters a verse that combined warning with sales pitch: "When lawless lust hath conceived it bringeth forth sin." Old and not quite sober, the cleric was nevertheless quick. Within minutes they were back in the wagon steeped in anticipation of a fresh bountiful life.

He seemed shy at first, so she thought he had not lived with eight people in a single room garret; had not grown so familiar with small cries of passion at dawn

that they were like the songs of peddlers. It was nothing
like what Dorothea had described or the acrobatics that
made Lydia hoot, nor like the quick and angry cou-
plings of her parents. Instead she felt not so much taken
as urged.

"My northern star," he called her.

They settled into the long learning of one another:
preferences, habits altered, others acquired; disagree-
ment without bile; trust and that wordless conversation
that years of companionship rest on. The weak religious
tendencies that riled Rebekka's mother were of no interest to him. He was indifferent, having himself with-
stood all pressure to join the village congregation but
content to let her be persuaded if she chose. After some
initial visits and Rebekka choosing not to continue, his
satisfaction was plain. They leaned on each other root
and crown. Needing no one outside their sufficiency. Or
so they believed. For there would be children, of course.
And there were. Following Patrician, each time Rebekka
gave birth, she forgot the previous nursing interrupted
long before weaning time. Forgot breasts still leaking, or
nipples prematurely caked and too tender for under-
clothes. Forgot, too, how rapid the trip from crib to coffin could be.

As the sons died and the years passed, Jacob became
convinced the farm was sustainable but not profitable.
He began to trade and travel. His returns, however, were
joyful times, full of news and amazing sights: the anger,
loud and lethal, of townspeople when a pastor was shot
dead off his horse by warriors of a local tribe; a shop's
shelves stacked with bolts of silk in colors he saw only in

nature; a freebooter tied to a plank on his way to the gallows cursing his captors in three languages; a butcher
thrashed for selling diseased meat; the eerie sounds of
choirs drifting in Sunday rain. Tales of his journeys
excited her, but also intensified her view of a disorderly,
threatening world out there, protection from which he
alone could provide. If on occasion he brought her
young, untrained help, he also brought home gifts. A
better chopping knife, a hobbyhorse for Patrician. It was
some time before she noticed how the tales were fewer
and the gifts increasing, gifts that were becoming less
practical, even whimsical. A silver tea service which was
put away immediately; a porcelain chamber pot quickly
chipped by indiscriminate use; a heavily worked hair-
brush for hair he only saw in bed. A hat here, a lace collar there. Four yards of silk. Rebekka swallowed her
questions and smiled. When finally she did ask him
where this money was coming from, he said, "New
arrangements," and handed her a mirror framed in silver. Having seen come and go a glint in his eye as he
unpacked these treasures so useless on a farm, she
should have anticipated the day he hired men to help
clear trees from a wide swath of land at the foot of a rise.
A new house he was building. Something befitting not a
farmer, not even a trader, but a squire.

We are good, common people, she thought, in a
place where that claim was not merely enough, but
prized, even a boast.

"We don't need another house," she told him. "Certainly not one of such size." She was shaving him and
spoke as she finished.

"Need is not the reason, wife."

"What is, pray?" Rebekka cleared off the last dollop of lather from the blade.

"What a man leaves behind is what a man is."

"Jacob, a man is only his reputation."

"Understand me." He took the cloth from her hands and wiped his chin. "I will have it."

And so it was. Men, barrows, a blacksmith, lumber, twine, pots of pitch, hammers and pull horses, one of which once kicked her daughter in the head. The fever of building was so intense she missed the real fever, the one that put him in the grave. As soon as he collapsed, word went out to the Baptists, and no one from the farm, especially Sorrow, was allowed among them. The laborers left with their horses and tools. The blacksmith was long gone, his ironwork aglitter like a gate to heaven. Rebekka did what Jacob ordered her to do: gathered the women and struggled with them to lift him from the bed and lower him onto a blanket. All the while he croaked, hurry, hurry. Unable to summon muscle strength to aid them, he was deadweight before he was dead. They hauled him through a cold spring rain. Skirts dragging in mud, shawls asunder, the caps on their heads drenched through to the scalp. There was trouble at the gate. They had to lay him in mud while two undid the hinges and then unbolted the door to the house. As rain poured over his face, Rebekka tried to shelter it with her own. Using the driest part of her underskirt, she blotted carefully lest she disturb the boils into pain. At last they entered the hall and situated him far away from the rain blowing through the window space. Rebekka leaned in close to ask if he would take a little cider. He moved his lips but no answer came. His eyes shifted to something or someone over her shoulder and remained so till she closed them. All four—herself, Lina, Sorrow and Florens—sat down on the floor planks. One or all thought the others were crying, or else those were raindrops on their cheeks.

Rebekka doubted that she would be infected. None of her parents' relatives had died during the pestilence; they boasted that no red cross had been painted on their door, although they saw hundreds and hundreds of dogs slaughtered and cartloads of the dead creaking by the commons. So to have sailed to this clean world, this fresh and new England, marry a stout, robust man and then, on the heels of his death, to lie festering on a perfect spring night felt like a jest. Congratulations, Satan. That was what the cutpurse used to say whenever the ship rose and threw their bodies helter-skelter.

"Blasphemy!" Elizabeth would shout.

"Truth!" Dorothea replied.

Now they hovered in the doorway or knelt by her bed.

"I'm already dead," said Judith. "It's not so bad."

"Don't tell her that. It's horrid."

"Don't listen to her. She's a pastor's wife now."

"Would you like some tea?"

"I married a sailor, so I'm always alone."

"She supplements his earnings. Ask her how."

"There are laws against that."

"Surely, but they would not have them if they did not need them."

"Listen, let me tell you what happened to me. I met this man. . . ."

Just as on the ship, their voices knocked against one another. They had come to soothe her but, like all ghostly presences, they were interested only in themselves. Yet the stories they told, their comments, offered Rebekka the distraction of other people's lives. Well, she thought, that was the true value of Job's comforters. He lay wracked with pain and in moral despair; they told him about themselves, and when he felt even worse, he got an answer from God saying, Who on earth do you think you are? Question me? Let me give you a hint of who I am and what I know. For a moment Job must have longed for the self-interested musings of humans as vulnerable and misguided as he was. But a peek into Divine knowledge was less important than gaining, at last, the Lord's attention. Which, Rebekka concluded, was all Job ever wanted. Not proof of His existence— he never questioned that. Nor proof of His power— everyone accepted that. He wanted simply to catch His eye. To be recognized not as worthy or worthless, but to be noticed as a life-form by the One who made and unmade it. Not a bargain; merely a glow of the miraculous.

But then Job was a man. Invisibility was intolerable to men. What complaint would a female Job dare to put forth? And if, having done so, and He deigned to remind her of how weak and ignorant she was, where was the news in that? What shocked Job into humility and renewed fidelity was the message a female Job would have known and heard every minute of her life. No. Better false comfort than none, thought Rebekka, and listened carefully to her shipmates.

"He knifed me, blood everywhere. I grabbed my
waist and thought, No! No swooning, my girl.
Steady. . . ."

When the women faded, it was the moon that stared
back like a worried friend in a sky the texture of a fine
lady's ball gown. Lina snored lightly on the floor at the
foot of the bed. At some point, long before Jacob's
death, the wide untrammeled space that once thrilled
her became vacancy. A commanding and oppressive
absence. She learned the intricacy of loneliness: the horror of color, the roar of soundlessness and the menace of
familiar objects lying still. When Jacob was away. When
neither Patrician nor Lina was enough. When the local
Baptists tired her out with talk that never extended
beyond their fences unless it went all the way to heaven.
Those women seemed flat to her, convinced they were
innocent and therefore free; safe because churched;
tough because still alive. A new people remade in vessels
old as time. Children, in other words, without the joy or
the curiosity of a child. They had even narrower defini-
tions of God's preferences than her parents. Other than
themselves (and those of their kind who agreed), no one
was saved. The possibility was open to most, however,
except children of Ham. In addition there were Papists
and the tribes of Judah to whom redemption was denied
along with a variety of others living willfully in error.
Dismissing these exclusions as the familiar restrictions
of all religions, Rebekka held a more personal grudge
against them. Their children. Each time one of hers
died, she told herself it was anti-baptism that enraged
her. But the truth was she could not bear to be around
their undead, healthy children. More than envy she felt

that each laughing red-cheeked child of theirs was an accusation of failure, a mockery of her own. Anyway, they were poor company and of no help to her with the solitude without prelude that could rise up and take her prisoner when Jacob was away. She might be bending in a patch of radishes, tossing weeds with the skill of a pub matron dropping coins into her apron. Weeds for the stock. Then as she stood in molten sunlight, pulling the corners of her apron together, the comfortable sounds of the farm would drop. Silence would fall like snow floating around her head and shoulders, spreading outward to wind-driven yet quiet leaves, dangling cowbells, the whack of Lina's axe chopping firewood nearby. Her skin would flush, then chill. Sound would return eventually, but the loneliness might remain for days. Until, in the middle of it, he would ride up shouting,

"Where's my star?"

"Here in the north," she'd reply and he would toss a bolt of calico at her feet or hand her a packet of needles. Best of all were the times when he would take out his pipe and embarrass the songbirds who believed they owned twilight. A still living baby would be on her lap. Patrician would be on the floor, mouth agape, eyes aglow, as he summoned rose gardens and shepherds neither had seen or would ever know. With him, the cost of a solitary, unchurched life was not high.

Once, feeling fat with contentment, she curbed her generosity, her sense of excessive well-being, enough to pity Lina.

"You have never known a man, have you?"

They were sitting in the brook, Lina holding the baby, splashing his back to hear him laugh. In frying

August heat they had taken the washing down to a part of the brook that swarming flies and vicious mosquitoes ignored. Unless a light canoe sailed by very close to the riverbank beyond no one would see them. Patrician knelt nearby watching how her bloomers stirred in the ripples. Rebekka sat in her underwear rinsing her neck and arms. Lina, naked as the baby she held in her arms, lifted him up and down watching his hair reshape itself in the current. Then she held him over her shoulder and sent cascades of clear water over his back.

"Known, Miss?"

"You understand me, Lina."

"I do."

"Well?"

"Look," squealed Patrician, pointing.

"Shhh," Lina whispered. "You will frighten them." Too late. The vixen and her kits sped away to drink elsewhere.

"Well?" Rebekka repeated. "Have you?"

"Once."

"And?"

"Not good. Not good, Miss."

"Why was that?"

"I will walk behind. I will clean up after. I will not be thrashed. No."

Handing the baby to his mother, Lina stood and walked to the raspberry bushes where her shift hung. Dressed, she cradled the laundry basket in her arm and held out a hand to Patrician.

Left alone with the baby who more than any of her children favored their father, Rebekka savored again on that day the miracle of her good fortune. Wife beating was common, she knew, but the restrictions—not after nine at night, with cause and not anger—were for wives and only wives. Had he been a native, Lina's lover? Probably not. A rich man? Or a common soldier or sailor? Rebekka suspected the rich man since she had known kind sailors but, based on her short employment as a kitchen maid, had seen only the underside of gentry. Other than her mother, no one had ever struck her. Fourteen years and she still didn't know if her mum was alive. She once received a message from a captain Jacob knew. Eighteen months after he was charged to make inquiries, he reported that her family had moved. Where, no one could say. Rising from the brook, laying her son in the warm grass while she dressed, Rebekka had wondered what her mother might look like now. Gray, stooped, wrinkled? Would the sharp pale eyes still radiate the shrewdness, the suspicion, Rebekka hated? Or maybe age, illness, had softened her to benign, toothless malice.

Confined to bed now, her question was redirected. "And me? How do I look? What lies in my eyes now? Skull and crossbones? Rage? Surrender?" All at once she wanted it—the mirror Jacob had given her which she had silently rewrapped and tucked in her press. It took a while to convince her, but when Lina finally understood and fixed it between her palms, Rebekka winced.

"Sorry," she murmured. "I'm so sorry." Her eyebrows were a memory, the pale rose of her cheeks collected now into buds of flame red. She traveled her face slowly, gently apologizing. "Eyes, dear eyes, forgive me. Nose, poor mouth. Poor, sweet mouth, I'm sorry. Believe me, skin, I do apologize. Please. Forgive me."

Lina, unable to pry the mirror away, was pleading with her.

"Miss. Enough. Enough."

Rebekka refused and clung to the mirror.

Oh, she had been so happy. So hale. Jacob home and busy with plans for the new house. The evenings when he was exhausted and she picked his hair clean; the mornings when she tied it. She loved his voracious appetite and the pride he took in her cooking. The blacksmith, who worried everybody except herself and Jacob, was like an anchor holding the couple in place in untrustworthy waters. Lina was afraid of him. Sorrow grateful as a hound to him. And Florens, poor Florens, she was completely smitten. Of the three, only she could be counted on to get to him. Lina would have begged off, unwilling to leave her patient, of course, but, more than that, despising him. Pregnant stupid Sorrow could not have. Rebekka had confidence in Florens because she was clever and because she had a strong reason to succeed. And she felt a lot of affection for her, although it took some time to develop. Jacob probably believed giving her a girl close to Patrician's age would please her. In fact, it insulted her. Nothing could replace the original and nothing should. So she barely glanced at her when she came and had no need to later because Lina took the child so completely under her wing. In time, Rebekka thawed, relaxed, was even amused by Florens' eagerness for approval. "Well done." "It's fine." However slight, any kindness shown her she munched like a rabbit. Jacob said the mother had no use for her which, Rebekka decided, explained her need to please. Explained also her attachment to the blacksmith, trotting up to him for any reason, panicked to get his food to him on time. Jacob dismissed Lina's glower and Florens' shine: the blacksmith would soon be gone, he said. No need to worry, besides the man was too skilled and valuable to let go, certainly not because a girl was mooning over him. Jacob was right, of course. The smithy's value was without price when he cured Sorrow of whatever had struck her down. Pray to God he could repeat that miracle. Pray also Florens could persuade him. They'd stuffed her feet in good strong boots. Jacob's. And folded a clarifying letter of authority inside. And her traveling instructions were clear.

It would all be all right. Just as the pall of childlessness coupled with bouts of loneliness had disappeared, melted like the snow showers that signaled it. Just as Jacob's determination to rise up in the world had ceased to trouble her. She decided that the satisfaction of having more and more was not greed, was not in the things themselves, but in the pleasure of the process. Whatever the truth, however driven he seemed, Jacob was there. With her. Breathing next to her in bed. Reaching for her even as he slept. Then suddenly, he was not.

Were the Anabaptists right? Was happiness Satan's allure, his tantalizing deceit? Was her devotion so frail it was merely bait? Her stubborn self-sufficiency outright blasphemy? Is that why at the height of her contentedness, once again death turned to look her way? And smile? Well, her shipmates, it seemed, had got on with it. As she knew from their visits, whatever life threw up, whatever obstacles they faced, they manipulated the circumstances to their advantage and trusted their own imagination. The Baptist women trusted elsewhere. Unlike her shipmates, they neither dared nor stood up to the fickleness of life. On the contrary, they dared death. Dared it to erase them, to pretend this earthly life was all; that beyond it was nothing; that there was no acknowledgment of suffering and certainly no reward; they refused meaninglessness and the random. What excited and challenged her shipmates horrified the churched women and each set believed the other deeply, dangerously flawed. Although they had nothing in common with the views of each other, they had everything in common with one thing: the promise and threat of men. Here, they agreed, was where security and risk lay. And both had come to terms. Some, like Lina, who had experienced both deliverance and destruction at their hands, withdrew. Some, like Sorrow, who apparently was never coached by other females, became their play. Some like her shipmates fought them. Others, the pious, obeyed them. And a few, like herself, after a mutually loving relationship, became like children when the man was gone. Without the status or shoulder of a man, without the support of family or well-wishers, a widow was in practice illegal. But was that not the way it should be? Adam first, Eve next, and also, confused about her role, the first outlaw?

The Anabaptists were not confused about any of this. Adam (like Jacob) was a good man but (unlike Jacob) he had been goaded and undermined by his mate. They understood, also, that there were lines of acceptable behavior and righteous thought. Levels of sin, in other words, and lesser peoples. Natives and

Africans, for instance, had access to grace but not to heaven—a heaven they knew as intimately as they knew their own gardens. Afterlife was more than Divine; it was thrill-soaked. Not a blue and gold paradise of twenty-four-hour praise song, but an adventurous real life, where all choices were perfect and perfectly executed. How had the churchwoman she spoke to described it? There would be music and feasts; picnics and hayrides. Frolicking. Dreams come true. And perhaps if one was truly committed, consistently devout, God would take pity and allow her children, though too young for a baptism of full immersion, entrance to His sphere. But of greatest importance, there was time. All of it. Time to converse with the saved, laugh with them. Skate, even, on icy ponds with a crackling fire ashore to warm one's hands. Sleighs jingled and children made snow houses and played with hoops in the meadow because the weather would be whatever you wanted it to be. Think of it. Just imagine. No illness. Ever. No pain. No aging or frailty of any kind. No loss or grief or tears. And obviously no more dying, not even if the stars shattered into motes and the moon disintegrated like a corpse beneath the sea.

She had only to stop thinking and believe. The dry tongue in Rebekka's mouth behaved like a small animal that had lost its way. And though she understood that her thoughts were disorganized, she was also convinced of their clarity. That she and Jacob could once talk and argue about these things made his loss intolerable. Whatever his mood or disposition, he had been the true meaning of mate.

Now, she thought, there is no one except servants.

The best husband gone and buried by the women he left behind; children rose-tinted clouds in the sky. Sorrow frightened for her own future if I die, as she should be, a slow-witted girl warped from living on a ghost ship. Only Lina was steady, unmoved by any catastrophe as though she has seen and survived everything. As in that second year when Jacob was away, caught in an off-season blizzard, and she, Lina and Patrician after two days were close to starvation. No trail or road passable. Patrician turning blue in spite of the miserable dung fire sputtering in a hole in the dirt floor. It was Lina who dressed herself in hides, carried a basket and an axe, braved the thigh-high drifts, the mind-numbing wind, to get to the river. There she pulled from below the ice enough broken salmon to bring back and feed them. She filled her basket with all she could snare; tied the basket handle to her braid to keep her hands from freezing on the trek back.

That was Lina. Or was it God? Here in an abyss of loss, she wondered if the journey to this land, the dying off of her family, her whole life, in fact, were way-stations marking a road to revelation. Or perdition? How would she know? And now with death's lips calling her name, to whom should she turn? A blacksmith? Florens?

How long will it take will he be there will she get lost will someone assault her will she return will he and is it already too late? For salvation.

I sleep then wake to any sound. Then I am dreaming
cherry trees walking toward me. I know it is dreaming
because they are full in leaves and fruit. I don't know
what they want. To look? To touch? One bends down
and I wake with a little scream in my mouth. Nothing is
different. The trees are not heavy with cherries nor
nearer to me. I quiet down. That is a better dream than
a minha mãe standing near with her little boy. In those
dreams she is always wanting to tell me something. Is
stretching her eyes. Is working her mouth. I look away
from her. My next sleeping is deep.

Not birdsong but sunlight wakes me. All snow is
gone. Relieving myself is troublesome. Then I am going
north I think but maybe west also. No, north until I
come to where the brush does not let me through without clutching me and taking hold. Brambles spread

among saplings are wide and tall to my waist. I press through and through for a long time which is good since in front of me sudden is an open meadow wild with sunshine and smelling of fire. This is a place that remembers the burning of itself. New grass is underfoot, deep, thick, tender as lamb's wool. I stoop to touch it and remember how Lina loves to unravel my hair. It makes her laugh, saying it is proof I am in truth a lamb. And you, I ask her. A horse she answers and tosses her mane. It is hours I walk this sunny field, my thirst so loud I am faint. Beyond I see a light wood of birch and apple trees. The shade in there is green with young leaves. Bird talk is everyplace. I am eager to enter because water may be there. I stop. I hear hoofbeats. From among the trees riders clop toward me. All male, all native, all young. Some look younger than me. None have saddles on their horses. None. I marvel at that and the glare of their skin but I have fear of them too. They rein in close. They circle. They smile. I am shaking. They wear soft shoes but their horses are not shod and the hair of both boys and horses is long and free like Lina's. They talk words I don't know and laugh. One pokes his fingers in his mouth, in out, in out. Others laugh more. Him too. Then he lifts his head high, opens wide his mouth and directs his thumb to his lips. I drop to my knees in misery and fright. He dismounts and comes close. I smell the perfume of his hair. His eyes are slant, not big and round like Lina's. He grins while removing a pouch hanging from a cord across his chest. He holds it out to me but I am too trembling to reach so he drinks from it and offers it again. I want it am dying for it but I cannot move. What I am able to do is make my mouth wide. He steps closer and pours the water as I gulp it. One of the others says baa baa baa like a goat kid and they all laugh and slap their legs. The one pouring closes his pouch and after watching me wipe my chin returns it to his shoulder. Then he reaches into a belt hanging from his waist and draws out a dark strip, hands it to me, chomping his teeth. It looks like leather but I take it. As soon as I do he runs and leaps on his horse. I am shock. Can you believe this. He runs on grass and flies up to sit astride his horse. I blink and they all disappear. Where they once are is nothing. Only apple trees aching to bud and an echo of laughing boys.

I put the dark strip on my tongue and I am correct. It is leather. Yet salty and spicy giving much comfort to your girl.

Once more I aim north through the wood following at a distance the hoofprints of the boys' horses. It is warm and becoming warmer. Yet the earth is ever moist with cool dew. I make me forget how we are on wet ground and think instead of fireflies in tall dry grass. There are so many stars it is like the day. You hold your hand over my mouth so no one can hear my pleasure startling hens from their sleep. Quiet. Quiet. No one must know but Lina does. Beware she tells me. We are lying in hammocks. I am just come from you aching with sin and looking forward to more. I ask her meaning. She says there is only one fool in this place and she is not it so beware. I am too sleepy to answer and not wanting to. I prefer thoughts of that place under your jaw where your neck meets bone, a small curve deep

enough for a tongue tip but no bigger than a quail's egg.
I am sinking into sleep when I hear her say, rum I told
myself it was rum. Only rum the first time because a
man of his learning and position in the town would
never dishonor himself so if sober. I understand, she is
saying, I understand and obey the need for secrecy and
when he comes to the house I never look him in the eye.
I only look for the straw in his mouth, she is saying, or
the stick he places in the gate hinge as the sign of our
meeting that night. Sleepiness is leaving me. I sit up and
dangle my legs over the hammock. The ropes creak and
sway. There is something in her voice that pricks me.
Something old. Something cutting. I look at her.
Brightness of stars, moon glow, both are enough to see
her face but neither is enough to know her expression.
Her braid is loose, strands of it escaping the hammock's
weave. She is saying that she is without clan and under a
Europe's rule. There is no rum the second time nor the
next, she is saying, but those times he uses the flat of his
hand when he has anger, when she spills lamp oil on his
breeches or he finds a tiny worm in the stew. Then
comes a day when he uses first his fist and then a whip.
The Spanish coin is lost through a worn place in her
apron pocket and is never found. He cannot forgive
this. I am already fourteen and ought to know better,
she is saying. And now, she is saying, I do. She tells me
how it is to walk town lanes wiping blood from her nose
with her fingers, that because her eyes are closing she
stumbles and people believe she is in liquor like so many
natives and tell her so. The Presbyterians stare at her face
and the blood wipes on her clothes but say nothing.

They visit the printer and offer her up for sale. They no longer let her inside their house so for weeks she sleeps where she can and eats from the bowl they leave for her on the porch. Like a dog, she says. Like a dog. Then Sir makes the purchase but not before she slips away and breaks the necks of two roosters and places a head in each of her lover's shoes. Every step he takes from then on will bring him closer to perpetual ruin.

Listen to me, she is saying. I am your age when flesh is my only hunger. Men have two hungers. The beak that grooms also bites. Tell me, she says, what will it be when his work here is done. I wonder she says will he take you with him?

I am not wondering this. Not then, not ever. I know you cannot steal me nor wedding me. Neither one is lawful. What I know is that I wilt when you go and am straight when Mistress sends me to you. Being on an errand is not running away.

Thinking these things keeps me walking and not lying down on the ground and allowing myself to sleep. I am greatly tired and long for water.

I come into a part where cows are grazing among the trees. If cows are in the woods a farm or village is near. Neither Sir nor Mistress will let their few heads loose like that. They fence the meadow because they want the manure and not a quarrel with neighbors. Mistress says Sir says grazing will soon die in the meadow so he has other business because farming will never be enough in these parts. Black flies alone will kill all hope for it if marauding wildlife does not. Farms live or die by the desire of insects or on the whim of weather.

I see a path and enter. It leads to a narrow bridge past a mill wheel poised in a stream. The creaking wheel and rushing water are what shape the quiet. Hens sleep and dogs forbidden. I hurry down the bank and lap from the stream. The water tastes like candle wax. I spit out the bits of straw that come with each swallow and make my way back to the path. I need shelter. The sun is setting itself. I notice two cottages. Both have windows but no lamp shines through. There are more that resemble small barns that can accept the day's light only through open doors. None is open. There is no cooksmoke in the air. I am thinking everyone has gone off. Then I see a tiny steeple on a hill beyond the village and am certain the people are at evening prayer. I decide to knock on the door of the largest house, the one that will have a servant inside. Moving toward it I look over my shoulder and see a light farther on. It is in the single lit house in the village so I choose to go there. Stones interfere at each step rubbing the sealing wax hard into my sole. Rain starts. Soft. It should smell sweet with the flavor of the sycamores it has crossed, but it has a burn smell, like pinfeathers singed before boiling a fowl.

Soon as I knock a woman opens the door. She is much taller than Mistress or Lina and has green eyes. The rest of her is a brown frock and a white cap. Red hair edges it. She is suspicious and holds up her hand, palm out, as though I might force my way in. Who hath sent you she asks. I say please. I say I am alone. No one sends me. Shelter calls me here. She looks behind me left and right and asks if I have no protection, no companion? I say No Madam. She narrows her eyes and asks

if I am of this earth or elsewhere? Her face is hard. I say
this earth Madam I know no other. Christian or heathen, she asks. Never heathen I say. I say although I hear
my father may be. And where doth he abide, she asks.
The rain is getting bigger. Hunger wobbles me. I say I
do not know him and my mother is dead. Her face soft-
ens and she nods saying, orphan, step in.

She tells me her name, Widow Ealing, but does not
ask mine. You must excuse me, she says, but there is
some danger about. What danger I ask. Evil, she says,
but you must never mind.

I try to eat slowly and fail. Sopping hard bread into
lovely, warm barley porridge, I don't lift my head except
to say thank you when she ladles more into my bowl.
She places a handful of raisins next to it. We are in a
good-size room with fireplace, table, stools and two
sleeping places, a box bed and a pallet. There are two
closed doors to other parts and a closet-looking place, a
niche, at the rear where jugs and bowls are. When my
hunger is quiet enough I notice a girl lying in the straw
of the box bed. Under her head is a blanket roll. One of
her eyes looks away, the other is as straight and unwaver-
ing as a she-wolf's. Both are black as coal, not at all like
the Widow's. I don't think I should begin any words so I
keep eating and wait for the girl or the Widow to say
something. At the foot of her bed is a basket. A kid lies
there too sick to raise its head or make a sound. When I
finish the food down to the last raisin the Widow asks
what is my purpose traveling alone. I tell her my mistress is sending me on an errand. She turns her lips
down saying it must be vital to risk a female's life in

these parts. My mistress is dying I say. My errand can save her. She frowns and looks toward the fireplace. Not from the first death, she says. Perhaps from the second.

I don't understand her meaning. I know there is only one death not two and many lives beyond it. Remember the owls in daylight? We know right away who they are. You know the pale one is your father. I think I know who the other ones may be.

The girl lying in straw raises up on her elbow. This be the death we have come here to die, she says. Her voice is deep, like a man's, though she looks to have my age. Widow Ealing doesn't reply and I do not want to look at those eyes anymore. The girl speaks again. No thrashing, she says, can change it, though my flesh is cut to ribbons. She stands then and limps to the table where the lamp burns. Holding it waist high she lifts her skirts. I see dark blood beetling down her legs. In the light pouring over her pale skin her wounds look like live jewels.

This is my daughter Jane, the Widow says. Those lashes may save her life.

It is late, Widow Ealing is saying. They will not come until morning. She closes the shutters, blows out the lamp and kneels by the pallet. Daughter Jane returns to her straw. The Widow whispers in prayer. The dark in here is greater than the cowshed, thicker than the forest. No moonlight seeps through a single crack. I lie near the sick kid and the fireplace and my sleep breaks into pieces from their voices. Silence is long and then they talk. I can tell who it is not only by the direction of the sound but also because Widow Ealing says words in a way different from her daughter. A more singing way. So I know it is Daughter Jane who says how can I prove I am not a demon and it is the Widow who says sssst it is they who will decide. Silence. Silence. Then back and forth they talk. It is the pasture they crave, Mother. Then why not me? You may be next. At least two say they have seen the Black Man and that he . . . Widow Ealing stops and does not say more for a while and then she says we will know comes the morning. They will allow that I am, says Daughter Jane. They talk fast to each other. The knowing is theirs, the truth is mine, truth is God's, then what mortal can judge me, you talk like a Spaniard, listen, please listen, be still lest He hear you, He will not abandon me, nor will I, yet you bloodied my flesh, how many times do you have to hear it demons do not bleed.

You never tell me that and it is a good thing to know. If my mother is not dead she can be teaching me these things.

I believe I am the only one who falls asleep and I wake in shame because outside the animals are already lowing. Tiny baas come from the kid as the Widow picks it up in her arms and takes it outside to nurse the dam. When she returns she unshutters both windows and leaves the door wide open. Two geese waddle in followed by a strutting hen. Another flies through a window joining the search for scraps. I ask permission to use the commode behind a hempen curtain. As I finish and step out I see Daughter Jane holding her face in her hands while the Widow freshens the leg wounds. New strips of blood gleam among the dry ones. A goat steps in and moves toward the straw nibbling nibbling while Daughter Jane whimpers. After the bloodwork is done to her satisfaction the Widow pushes the goat out the door.

At table for a breakfast of clabber and bread the Widow and Daughter Jane put their palms together, bow their heads and murmur. I do likewise, whispering the prayer Reverend Father taught me to say morning and night my mother repeating with me. Pater Noster. . . . At the end I raise my hand to touch my forehead and catch Daughter Jane's frown. She shakes her head meaning no. So I pretend I am adjusting my cap. The Widow spoons jam onto the clabber and we two eat. Daughter Jane refuses so we eat what she will not. Afterwards the Widow goes to the fireplace and swings the kettle over the fire. I take the bowls and spoons from the table to the closet where a basin of water sits on a narrow bench. I rinse and wipe each piece carefully. The air is tight. Water rises to a boil in the kettle hanging in the fireplace. I turn and see its steam forming shapes as it curls against the stone. One shape looks like the head of a dog.

We all hear footsteps climbing the path. I am still busy in the closet, and although I cannot see who enters, I hear the talk. The Widow offers the visitors seating. They refuse. A man's voice says this is preliminary yet witnesses are several. Widow interrupts him saying her daughter's eye is askew as God made it and it has no special powers. And look, she says, look at her wounds. God's son bleeds. We bleed. Demons never.

I step into the room. Standing there are a man, three

women and a little girl who reminds me of myself when
my mother sends me away. I am thinking how sweet she
seems when she screams and hides behind the skirts of
one of the women. Then each visitor turns to look at
me. The women gasp. The man's walking stick clatters
to the floor causing the remaining hen to squawk and
flutter. He retrieves his stick, points it at me saying who
be this? One of the women covers her eyes saying God
help us. The little girl wails and rocks back and forth.
The Widow waves both hands saying she is a guest seek-
ing shelter from the night. We accept her how could we
not and feed her. Which night the man asks. This one
past she answers. One woman speaks saying I have never
seen any human this black. I have says another, this one
is as black as others I have seen. She is Afric. Afric and
much more, says another. Just look at this child says the
first woman. She points to the little girl shaking and
moaning by her side. Hear her. Hear her. It is true then
says another. The Black Man is among us. This is his
minion. The little girl is inconsolable. The woman
whose skirts she clings to takes her outside where she is
quickly quiet. I am not understanding anything except
that I am in danger as the dog's head shows and Mistress
is my only defense. I shout, wait. I shout, please sir. I
think they have shock that I can talk. Let me show you
my letter I say quieter. It proves I am nobody's minion
but my Mistress. As fast as I can I remove my boot and
roll down my stocking. The women stretch their
mouths, the man looks away and then slowly back. I
pull out Mistress' letter and offer it but no one will
touch it. The man orders me to place it on the table but

he is afraid to break the seal. He tells the Widow to do it. She picks at the wax with her fingernails. When it falls away she unfolds the paper. It is too thick to stay flat by itself. Everyone including Daughter Jane who rises from her bed stares at the markings upside down and it is clear only the man is lettered. Holding the tip of his walking stick down on the paper he turns it right side up and holds it there as if the letter can fly away or turn into ashes without flame before his eyes. He leans low and examines it closely. Then he picks it up and reads aloud.

> *The signatory of this letter, Mistress Rebekka Vaark of Milton vouches for the female person into whose hands it has been placed. She is owned by me and can be knowne by a burne mark in the palm of her left hand. Allow her the courtesie of safe passage and witherall she may need to complete her errand. Our life, my life, on this earthe depends on her speedy return.*
> *Signed Rebekka Vaark, Mistress, Milton*
> *18 May 1690*

Other than a small sound from Daughter Jane all is quiet. The man looks at me, looks again at the letter, back at me back at the letter. Again at me, once more at the letter. You see, says the Widow. He ignores her and turns to two women whispering to them. They point me to a door that opens onto a storeroom and there, standing among carriage boxes and a spinning wheel, they tell me to take off my clothes. Without touching they tell me what to do. To show them my teeth, my tongue. They frown at the candle burn on my palm, the one you kissed to cool. They look under my arms, between my legs. They circle me, lean down to inspect my feet. Naked under their examination I watch for what is in their eyes. No hate is there or scare or disgust but they are looking at me my body across distances without recognition. Swine look at me with more connection when they raise their heads from the trough. The women look away from my eyes the way you say I am to do with the bears so they will not come close to love and play. Finally they tell me to dress and leave the room shutting the door behind them. I put on my clothes. I hear the quarreling. The little girl is back, not sobbing now but saying it scares me it scares me. A woman's voice asks would Satan write a letter. Lucifer is all deceit and trickery says another. But a woman's life is at stake says the Widow, who will the Lord punish then? The man's voice booms. We will relay this to the others he says. We will study on it, consult and pray and return with our answer. It is not clear it seems whether or no I am the Black Man's minion. I step into the room and the little girl screams and flails her arms. The women surround her and rush out. The man says not to leave the house. He takes the letter with him. The Widow follows him down the path pleading, pleading.

She returns to say they are wanting time to discuss more among themselves. She has hope because of the letter. Daughter Jane laughs. Widow Ealing kneels to pray. She prays a long time then stands saying I have to see someone. I need his witness and his help.

Who, asks Daughter Jane.

The sheriff says the Widow.

Daughter Jane curls her mouth behind her mother's back as she leaves.

I am hung with fear watching Daughter Jane attend her leg wounds. The sun is high and still the Widow does not return. We wait. By and by the sun slows down. Daughter Jane boils duck eggs and when cool wraps them in a square of cloth. She folds a blanket and hands it to me, motions with one finger to follow. We leave the house, scurry around to the back. All manner of fowl cluck and fly from our feet. We run through the pasture. The nanny goat turns to look. The billy does not. A bad sign. We squeeze between the fence slats and run into the wood. Now we walk, softly, Daughter Jane leading the way. The sun empties itself, pouring what is left through tree shadow. Birds and small animals eat and call to one another.

We come to a stream, dry mostly, muddy elsewhere. Daughter Jane hands me the cloth of eggs. She explains how I am to go, where the trail will be that takes me to the post road that takes me to the hamlet where I hope you are. I say thank you and lift her hand to kiss it. She says no, I thank you. They look at you and forget about me. She kisses my forehead then watches as I step down into the stream's dry bed. I turn and look up at her. Are you a demon I ask her. Her wayward eye is steady. She smiles. Yes, she says. Oh, yes. Go now.

I walk alone except for the eyes that join me on my journey. Eyes that do not recognize me, eyes that examine me for a tail, an extra teat, a man's whip between my legs. Wondering eyes that stare and decide if my navel is in the right place if my knees bend backward like the forelegs of a dog. They want to see if my tongue is split like a snake's or if my teeth are filing to points to chew them up. To know if I can spring out of the darkness and bite. Inside I am shrinking. I climb the streambed under watching trees and know I am not the same. I am losing something with every step I take. I can feel the drain. Something precious is leaving me. I am a thing apart. With the letter I belong and am lawful. Without it I am a weak calf abandon by the herd, a turtle without shell, a minion with no telltale signs but a darkness I am born with, outside, yes, but inside as well and the inside dark is small, feathered and toothy. Is that what my mother knows? Why she chooses me to live without? Not the outside dark we share, a minha mãe and me, but the inside one we don't. Is this dying mine alone? Is the clawing feathery thing the only life in me? You will tell me. You have the outside dark as well. And when I see you and fall into you I know I am live. Sudden it is not like before when I am always in fright. I am not afraid of anything now. The sun's going leaves darkness behind and the dark is me. Is we. Is my home.

She did not mind when they called her Sorrow so long as Twin kept using her real name. It was easy to be confused. Sometimes it was the housewife or the sawyer or the sons who needed her; other times Twin wanted company to talk or walk or play. Having two names was convenient since Twin couldn't be seen by anybody else. So if she were scrubbing clothes or herding geese and heard the name Captain used, she knew it was Twin. But if any voice called "Sorrow," she knew what to expect. Preferable, of course, was when Twin called from the mill door or whispered up close into her ear. Then she would quit any chore and follow her identical self.

They had met beneath the surgeon's hammock in the looted ship. All people were gone or drowned and she might have been too had she not been deep in an opium sleep in the ship's surgery. Taken there to have the boils removed from her neck, she drank the mixture the surgeon said would cut off the pain. So when the ship foundered she did not know it, and if any unmurdered hands and passengers escaped, she didn't know that either. What she remembered was waking up after falling to the floor under the hammock all alone. Captain, her father, nowhere.

Before coming to the sawyer's house, Sorrow had never lived on land. Now the memories of the ship, the only home she knew, seemed as stolen as its cargo: bales of cloth, chests of opium, crates of ammunition, horses and barrels of molasses. Even the trace of Captain was dim. After searching for survivors and food, fingering spilt molasses from the deck straight into her mouth, nights listening to cold wind and lapping sea, Twin joined her under the hammock and they have been together ever since. Both skinned down the broken mast and started walking a rocky shoreline. The bits of dead fish they ate intensified their thirst which they forgot at the sight of two bodies rocking in the surf. It was the bloat and sway that made them incautious enough to wade away from the rocks into a lagoon just when the tide was coming in. Both were swept out to deep water; both treaded as long as they could until the cold overcame their senses and they swam not landward, but toward the horizon. Very good luck, for they entered a neap rushing headlong toward shore and into a river beyond.

Sorrow woke up naked under a blanket, with a warm wet cloth on her forehead. The smell of milled wood was overwhelming. A woman with white hair was watching her.

"Such a sight," said the woman, shaking her head.

"Such a dismal sight you are. Yet strong, I think, for a maid." She pulled the blanket up to the castaway's chin. "We thought from your clothes you were a lad. However, you're not dead."

That was good news, because Sorrow thought she was until Twin appeared at the foot of the pallet, grinning, holding her face in her hands. Comforted, Sorrow slept again, but easy now with Twin nestling near.

The next morning she woke to the grating of saws and the even thicker odor of wood chips. The sawyer's wife came in holding a man's shirt and a boy's breeches.

"These will have to do for now," she said. "I'll have to make you something more fitting for there is nothing to borrow in the village. And there won't be any shoes for a while."

Light-headed and wobbly, Sorrow put on the dry boy clothes, then followed a scent of food. Once fed an extravagant breakfast, she was alert enough to say things but not recall things. When they asked her name, Twin whispered NO, so she shrugged her shoulders and found that a convenient gesture for the other information she could not or pretended not to remember.

Where do you live?

On the ship.

Yes, but not always.

Always.

Where is your family?

Shoulders lifted.

Who else was on the ship?

Gulls.

What people, girl?

Shrug.

Who was the captain?

Shrug.

Well, how did you get to land?

Mermaids. I mean whales.

That was when the housewife named her. Next day
she gave her a shift of sacking, a clean cap to cover her
unbelievable and slightly threatening hair, and told her
to mind the geese. Toss their grain, herd them to water
and keep them from waddling off. Sorrow's bare feet
fought with the distressing gravity of land. She stumbled and tripped so much on that first day at the pond
that when two goslings were attacked by a dog and
chaos followed, it took forever to regroup the flock. She
kept at it a few more days, until the housewife threw up
her hands and put her to simple cleaning tasks—none
of which proved satisfactory. But the pleasure of up-
braiding an incompetent servant outweighed any satisfaction of a chore well done and the housewife raged
happily at every unswept corner, poorly made fire,
imperfectly scrubbed pot, carelessly weeded garden row
and badly plucked bird. Sorrow concentrated on meal-
times and the art of escape for short walks with Twin,
playtimes between or instead of her tasks. On occasion
she had secret company other than Twin, but not better
than Twin, who was her safety, her entertainment, her
guide.

The housewife told her it was monthly blood; that
all females suffered it and Sorrow believed her until the
next month and the next and the next when it did not
return. Twin and she talked about it, about whether it
was instead the result of the goings that took place
behind the stack of clapboard, both brothers attending,

instead of what the housewife said. Because the pain was outside between her legs, not inside where the house-wife said was natural. The hurt was still there when the sawyer asked Sir to take her away, saying his wife could not keep her.

Sir asked, "Where is she?" and Sorrow was summoned into the mill.

"How old?"

When the sawyer shook his head, Sorrow spoke up. "I believe I have eleven years now."

Sir grunted.

"Don't mind her name," said the sawyer. "You can name her anything you want. My wife calls her Sorrow because she was abandoned. She is a bit mongrelized as you can see. However be that, she will work without complaint."

As he spoke Sorrow saw the side smile on his face.

She rode behind Sir's saddle for miles with one stop on the way. Since it was her first time astride a horse, the burning brought her to tears. Swaying, bumping, cling-ing to Sir's coat, finally she threw up on it. He reined in, then, and lifted her down, letting her rest while he wiped his coat with a leaf of coltsfoot. She accepted his water pouch, but the first gulp spewed out along with whatever was left in her stomach.

"Sorrow, indeed," mumbled Sir.

She was grateful when they got close to his farm and he took her down so she could walk the rest of the way. He looked around every few furlongs to make sure she had not fallen or sickened again.

Twin smiled and clapped her hands when they

glimpsed the farm. All along the trail riding behind Sir, Sorrow had looked around with a fright that would have been even deeper had she not been suffering nausea as well as pain. Miles of hemlock towered like black ship masts, and when they fell away cathedral pine, thick as the horse was long, threw shadows over their heads. No matter how she tried, she never saw their tops that, for all she knew, broke open the sky. Now and again a hulking pelted shape standing among the trees watched them ride by. Once when an elk crossed their path, Sir had to swerve and turn the horse around four times before it would go forward again. So when she followed Sir's horse into a sun-drenched clearing and heard the cackle of ducks neither she nor Twin could have been more relieved. Unlike the housewife, Mistress and Lina both had small, straight noses; Mistress' skin was like the whites of eggs, Lina's like the brown of their shells. Before anything, food or rest, Lina insisted on washing Sorrow's hair. Not only the twigs and bits of straw hiding under her cap bothered her; she feared lice. It was a fear that surprised Sorrow who thought lice, like ticks, fleas or any of the other occupants of the body, were more nuisance than danger. Lina thought otherwise and after the hair-washing, scrubbed the girl down twice before letting her in the house. Then, shaking her head from side to side, gave her a salted rag to clean her teeth.

Sir, holding Patrician's hand, announced that she be confined to the house at night. When Mistress asked why, he said, "I'm told she wanders."

In the chill of that first night, scrunched on a mat

near the fireplace, Sorrow slept and woke, slept and woke, lulled continuously by Twin's voice describing the thousandfold men walking the waves, singing wordlessly. How their teeth glittered more than the whitecaps under their feet. How, as the sky darkened and the moon rose, the edges of their night-black skin silvered. How the smell of land, ripe and loamy, brightened the eyes of the crew but made the sea walkers cry. Soothed by Twin's voice and the animal fat Lina had spread on her lower parts, Sorrow fell into the first sweet sleep she had had in months.

Still, that first morning, she threw up her breakfast as soon as she swallowed. Mistress gave her yarrow tea and put her to work in the vegetable garden. Prying late turnips from the ground, she could hear Sir breaking rocks in a far-off field. Patrician squatted at the edge of the garden eating a yellow apple and watching her. Sorrow waved. Patrician waved back. Lina appeared and hurried the little girl away. From then on it was clear to Twin, if not to Sorrow, that Lina ruled and decided everything Sir and Mistress did not. Her eye was everywhere even when she was nowhere. She rose before cock crow, entered the house in darkness, touched a sleeping Sorrow with the toe of her moccasin and lingered while refreshing the embers. She examined baskets, looked under the lids of jars. Checking the stores, thought Sorrow. No, said Twin, checking you for food theft.

Lina spoke very little to her, not even "good morning," and only when the content of what she had to say was urgent. Therefore it was she who told Sorrow she was pregnant. Lina had removed a basket of millet from

Sorrow's hands. Looked her dead in the eye and said, "Do you know you are with child, child?"

Sorrow's jaw dropped. Then she flushed with pleasure at the thought of a real person, a person of her own, growing inside her.

"What should I do?" she asked.

Lina simply stared at her and, hoisting the basket on her hip, walked away. If Mistress knew, she never said, perhaps because she was pregnant herself. Sorrow's birthing came too soon, Lina told her, for the infant to survive, but Mistress delivered a fat boy who cheered everybody up—for six months anyway. They put him with his brother at the bottom of the rise behind the house and said prayers. Although Sorrow thought she saw her own newborn yawn, Lina wrapped it in a piece of sacking and set it a-sail in the widest part of the stream and far below the beavers' dam. It had no name. Sorrow wept, but Twin told her not to. "I am always with you," she said. That was some consolation, but it took years for Sorrow's steady thoughts of her baby breathing water under Lina's palm to recede. With no one to talk to, she relied on Twin more and more. With her, Sorrow never wanted for friendship or conversation. Even if they made her sleep inside, there were stories to listen to and they could steal away together during the day for strolls and larks in the forest. There were cherries, too, and walnuts from the deacon. But she had to be quiet. Once he brought her a neckerchief which she filled with stones and threw in the stream, knowing such finery would raise Lina's anger as well as alert Mistress. And although another of Mistress' baby boys perished, Patrician stayed healthy. For a little while Lina seemed to be persuaded that the boys' deaths were not Sorrow's fault, but when a horse broke Patrician's crown, she changed her mind.

Then came Florens.

Then came the blacksmith. Twice.

When Florens arrived that bitter winter, Sorrow, curious and happy to see someone new, smiled and was about to step forward just to touch one of the little girl's fat braids. But Twin stopped her, leaning close to Sorrow's face, crying, "Don't! Don't!" Sorrow recognized Twin's jealousy and waved her face away, but not quickly enough. Lina, having taken off her shawl and wrapped it around the child's shoulders, picked her up and carried her into the cowshed. Thereafter, the girl belonged to Lina. They slept together, bathed together, ate together. Lina made clothes for her and tiny shoes from rabbit skin. Whenever Sorrow came near, Lina said "Scat," or sent her on some task that needed doing immediately, all the while making certain everyone else shared the distrust that sparkled in her own eyes. Sorrow remembered how they narrowed, gleamed, when Sir made her sleep inside. And although Lina helped her through childbirth, Sorrow never forgot the baby breathing water every day, every night, down all the streams of the world. Kept as distant from the new girl as she had been from Patrician, Sorrow behaved thereafter the way she always had—with placid indifference to anyone, except Twin.

Years later, when the blacksmith came, the weather of the place changed. Forever. Twin noticed it first, saying Lina was afraid of the smithy and tried to warn Mistress about him, but the warning was fruitless. Mistress paid it no attention. She was too happy for guardedness because Sir was not traveling anymore. He was always there working on the new house, managing deliveries, laying string from angle to angle and in close conversation with the smithy about the gate's design. Lina dreading; Mistress humming with contentment; Sir in high spirits. Florens, of course, was the most distracted.

Neither Sorrow nor Twin had settled on exactly what to think of the blacksmith. He seemed complete, unaware of his effect. Was he the danger Lina saw in him or was her fear mere jealousy? Was he Sir's perfect building partner or a curse on Florens, altering her behavior from open to furtive? They had yet to make up their minds when Sorrow, returning from the stream with a bucket of water, collapsed, burning and shaking, near the building site. It was pure luck that the smithy was right there and saw her fall. He picked her up and laid her down on the pallet where he slept. Sorrow's face and arms were welting. The smithy touched her neck boils, then shouted. Sir poked his head out of the door frame and Florens came running. Mistress arrived and the smithy called for vinegar. Lina went to fetch it, and when it came, he doused Sorrow's boils and the skin of her face and arms, sending her into spasms of pain. While the women sucked air and Sir frowned, the blacksmith heated a knife and slit open one of the swellings. They watched in silence as he tipped Sorrow's own blood drops between her lips. All of them thought it better not to have her in the house, so Sorrow lay sweltering in a hammock all day, all night—permitted no food or water—as the women took turns fanning her. The constant breeze of their fans summoned sail wind and Captain, the tiller in his hand. She heard him before she saw him. Laughing. Loud, raucous. No. Not laughing. Screaming. Along with the others. High-pitched and low, the screams were far away, on the other side of the white clouds surrounding her. Horses, too. Pounding hooves. Freed from below. Leaping over sacks of grain and kicking barrels until the staves broke and a thick sweet blackness poured out. Still, she could not move or tear through the clouds. Pushing, pushing, she fell to the floor while the clouds covered and smothered her whole self, convincing her the screams belonged to gulls. When she came to, eyes, the shape and color of her own, greeted her. The puffy clouds, mere threads now, drifted away.

"I'm here," said the girl with a face matching her own exactly. "I'm always here."

With Twin she was less afraid and the two began to search the silent, listing ship. Slowly, slowly. Peeking here, listening there, finding nothing except a bonnet and seagulls pecking the remains of a colt.

Under the waving fan, drenched in sweat, Sorrow remembered freezing day after day on the ship. Other than icy wind, nothing stirred. Aft was the sea, fore a rocky beach below a cliff of stone and brush. Sorrow had never set foot on land and was terrified of leaving ship for shore. It was as foreign to her as ocean was to sheep. Twin made it possible. When they descended, the earth—mean, hard, thick, hateful—shocked her. That's when she understood Captain's choice to keep her aboard. He reared her not as a daughter but as a sort of crewman-to-be. Dirty, trousered, both wild and obedient with one important skill, patching and sewing sailcloth.

Mistress and Lina quarreled with the blacksmith about whether she should be forced to eat or drink, but he ruled, insisting she have nothing. Riveted by that hot knife and blood medicine, they deferred. Fanning and vinegar-soaked boils only. At the close of the third day, Sorrow's fever broke and she begged for water. The smithy held her head as she sipped from a dried squash gourd. Raising her eyes, she saw Twin seated in the branches above the hammock, smiling. Soon Sorrow said she was hungry. Bit by bit, under the smithy's care and Florens' nursing, the boils shriveled, the welts disappeared and her strength returned. Now their judgment was clear: the blacksmith was a savior. Lina, however, became truly ugly in her efforts to keep Florens away from the patient and the healer, muttering that she had seen this sickness before when she was a child, and that it would spread like mold to them all. But she lost the battle with Florens. By the time Sorrow recovered, Florens was struck down with another sickness much longer lasting and far more lethal.

It was while lying in the meadow at the forest's edge, listening to Twin tell a favorite story, the one about a school of fish girls with pearls for eyes and green-black locks of seaweed hair racing one another, riding the backs of a fleet of whales, that Sorrow first saw the smithy and Florens coiled around each other. Twin had just gotten to the part where seabirds, excited by the foam trailing the fleet like shooting stars, were joining the race, when Sorrow put a finger to her lips and pointed with another. Twin stopped speaking and looked. The blacksmith and Florens were rocking and, unlike female farm animals in heat, she was not standing quietly under the weight and thrust of the male. What Sorrow saw yonder in the grass under a hickory tree was not the silent submission to the slow goings behind a pile of wood or a hurried one in a church pew that Sorrow knew. This here female stretched, kicked her heels and whipped her head left, right, to, fro. It was a dancing. Florens rolled and twisted from her back to his. He hoisted her up against the hickory; she bent her head into his shoulder. A dancing. Horizontal one minute, another minute vertical.

Sorrow watched until it was over; until, stumbling like tired old people, they dressed themselves. It all ended when the blacksmith grabbed Florens' hair, yanked her head back to put his mouth on hers. Then they went off in different directions. It amazed her to see that. In all of the goings she knew, no one had ever kissed her mouth. Ever.

It was natural, once Sir was buried and Mistress fell ill, to send for the blacksmith. And he came. Alone. He gazed for a while at the great, new house before dismounting. Then he glanced at Sorrow's belly, then her eyes before handing her the reins. He turned to Lina.

"Lead me to her," he said.

Sorrow rushed back from tying the horse as fast as her weight let her and the three of them entered the house. He paused and, noticing the smell, looked into the pot of stewed mugwort and other bits of Lina's brew.

"How long has she been abed?"

"Five days," answered Lina.

He grunted and entered Mistress' bedroom. Lina and Sorrow watched him from the door as he sat on his haunches beside the sickbed.

"Thank you for coming," whispered Mistress. "Will you make me drink my own blood? I'm afraid there is none left. None that isn't polluted."

He smiled and stroked her face.

"Am I dying?" she asked.

He shook his head. "No. The sickness is dead. Not you."

Mistress closed her eyes. When she opened them they were glassy and she blotted them with the back of a bandaged hand. She thanked him again and again, then told Lina to prepare him something to eat. When he left the room, Lina followed. Sorrow, too, but not before turning back for a last look. That was when she saw Mistress toss off the bedsheet and go down on her knees. Sorrow watched as she used her teeth to loosen the wrappings on her hands, then press her palms together. Glancing around the room she was usually forbidden to enter, Sorrow noticed the clumps of hair stuck in the pillow's damp; noticed too how helpless-looking were the soles of Mistress' pale feet, protruding from the hem of her nightdress. On her knees, her head bowed, she seemed completely alone in the world. Sorrow understood that servants, however many, would not make a difference. Somehow their care and devotion did not matter to her. So Mistress had no one—no one at all. Except the One she was whispering to: "Thank you my Lord for the saving grace you have shown me."

Sorrow tiptoed away, out into the yard where pine-scented air erased the odor of the sickroom. Somewhere a woodpecker tapped. When hares bounded into the radish patch Sorrow thought to chase them but, exhausted by her weight, decided not to. Instead she sat down on the grass in the shade of the house, stroking the movements in her protruding stomach. Above her through the kitchen window she could hear the clatter of a knife, the shift of a cup or plate as the blacksmith ate. She knew Lina was there too, but she did not speak until the sound of a chair scraping announced that the smithy stood. Then Lina asked the questions Mistress had not.

"Where is she? Is she all right?"

"Certainly."

"When will she return? Who will bring her back?"

A silence too long for Lina.

"It is four days now. You can't keep her against her will."

"Why would I?"

"Then? Tell me!"

"When it suits her she will come."

Silence.

"You will stay the night?"

"Part of it. Much obliged for the meal."

With that he left. Passing by Sorrow, he answered her smile with another and strode up the rise to the new house. Slowly he stroked the ironwork, a curve here, a

join there, tested the gilt for flakes. Then he went to Sir's
grave and stood hatless before it. After a while he went
inside the empty house and shut its door behind him.

He did not wait for sunrise. Sleepless and uncom-
fortable, Sorrow stood in the doorway and watched him
ride off in pre-dawn darkness as serenely cheerful as a
colt. It was soon clear, however, that Lina remained in
despair. The questions plaguing her lodged in her eyes:
What was really happening to Florens? Was she coming
back? Was the blacksmith truthful? For all his kindness
and healing powers, Sorrow wondered if she had been
wrong about him and Lina right all along. Suffused with
the deep insight mothers-to-be claim, Sorrow doubted it.
He had saved her life with vinegar and her own blood;
had known right away Mistress' state and what solvent
to prescribe to lessen the scarring. Lina was simply wary
of anyone who came between herself and Florens.
Between tending Mistress' new requirements and scan-
ning the path for Florens, Lina had little time or inclination for anything else. Sorrow herself, unable to bend
down, lift anything weighty or even walk a hundred
yards without heavy breathing, was equally to blame for
what was happening to the farm. Goats wandered from
village yards and tore up both newly planted gardens.
Layers of insects floated in the water barrel no one had
remembered to cover. Damp laundry left too long in the
basket began to mold and neither of them returned to
the river to wash it again. Everything was in disarray.
The weather was warming, and as a result of the canceled visit of a neighbor's bull, no cow foaled. Acres and
acres needed turning; milk became clabber in the pan. A

fox pawed the hen yard whenever she liked and rats ate the eggs. Mistress would not recover soon enough to catch the heap the farm was falling into. And without her pet, Lina, the silent workhorse, seemed to have lost interest in everything, including feeding herself. Ten days' neglect and collapse was everywhere. So it was in the afternoon silence of a cool day in May, on an untended farm recently swathed in smallpox, that Sorrow's water broke, unleashing her panic. Mistress was not well enough to help her, and remembering the yawn, she did not trust Lina. Forbidden to enter the village, she had no choice. Twin was absent, strangely silent or hostile when Sorrow tried to discuss what to do, where to go. With a frail hope that Will and Scully would be stationed as usual on their fishing raft, she took a knife and a blanket to the riverbank the moment the first pain hit. She stayed there, alone, screeching when she had to, sleeping in between, until the next brute tear of body and breath. Hours, minutes, days— Sorrow could not tell how much time passed before the men heard her moans and poled their raft to the river's edge. They both understood Sorrow's plight as quickly as they would any creature about to foal. Clumsy a bit, their purpose confined to the survival of the new-born, they set to work. Kneeling in water as Sorrow pushed, they pulled, eased and turned the tiny form stuck between her legs. Blood and more swirled down to the river attracting young cod. When the baby, a girl, whimpered, Scully knifed the cord, then handed her to the mother who rinsed her, dabbing her mouth, ears and unfocused eyes. The men congratulated themselves

and offered to carry mother and child back to the farm-
house. Sorrow, repeating "thank you" with every breath,
declined. She wanted to rest and would make her own
way. Willard slapped Scully on the back of his head,
laughing.

"Right fine midwife, I'd say."

"No question," answered Scully as they waded back
to their raft.

Following the expulsion of afterbirth, Sorrow
wrapped her infant in the blanket and dozed off and on
for hours. At some point before sunset she roused to a
cry and squeezed her breasts until one delivered.
Although all her life she had been saved by men—
Captain, the sawyers' sons, Sir and now Will and
Scully—she was convinced that this time she had done
something, something important, by herself. Twin's
absence was hardly noticed as she concentrated on her
daughter. Instantly, she knew what to name her. Knew
also what to name herself.

Two days came and went. Lina hid her disgust with
Sorrow and her anxiety about Florens under a mask of
calm. Mistress said nothing about the baby, but sent for
a Bible and forbade anyone to enter the new house. At
one point, Sorrow, prompted by the legitimacy of her
new status as a mother, was bold enough to remark to
her Mistress, "It was good that the blacksmith came to
help when you were dying." Mistress stared at her.

"Ninny," she answered. "God alone cures. No man
has such power."

There had always been tangled strings among them.
Now they were cut. Each woman embargoed herself;

spun her own web of thoughts unavailable to anyone else. It was as though, with or without Florens, they were falling away from one another.

Twin was gone, traceless and unmissed by the only person who knew her. Sorrow's wandering stopped too. Now she attended routine duties, organizing them around her infant's needs, impervious to the complaints of others. She had looked into her daughter's eyes; saw in them the gray glisten of a winter sea while a ship sailed by-the-lee. "I am your mother," she said. "My name is Complete."

My journey to you is hard and long and the hurt of it is gone as soon as I see the yard, the forge, the little cabin where you are. I lose the fear that I may never again in this world know the sight of your welcoming smile or taste the sugar of your shoulder as you take me in your arms. The smell of fire and ash trembles me but it is the glee in your eyes that kicks my heart over. You are asking me how and how long and laughing at my clothes and the scratches everyplace. But when I answer your why, you frown. We settle, you do, and I agree because there is no other way. You will ride at once to Mistress but alone. I am to wait here you say. I cannot join you because it is faster without me. And there is another reason, you say. You turn your head. My eyes follow where you look.

This happens twice before. The first time it is me

peering around my mother's dress hoping for her hand
that is only for her little boy. The second time it is a
pointing screaming little girl hiding behind her mother
and clinging to her skirts. Both times are full of danger
and I am expel. Now I am seeing a little boy come in
holding a corn-husk doll. He is younger than everybody
I know. You reach out your forefinger toward him and
he takes hold of it. You say this is why I cannot travel
with you. The child you call Malaik is not to be left
alone. He is a foundling. His father is leaning over
the reins and the horse is continuing until it stops and
eats grass in the lane. People from the village come,
learn he is dead and find the boy sitting quietly in the
cart. No one knows who is the dead man and nothing in
his belongings can tell. You accept him until a future
when a townsman or magistrate places him, which may
be never because although the dead man's skin is rosy
the boy's is not. So maybe he is not a son at all. My
mouth goes dry as I wonder if you want him to be
yours.

I worry as the boy steps closer to you. How you offer
and he owns your forefinger. As if he is your future. Not
me. I am not liking how his eyes go when you send him
to play in the yard. But then you bathe my journey from
my face and arms and give me stew. It needs salt. The
pieces of rabbit are thick and tender. My hunger is sharp
but my happiness is more. I cannot eat much. We talk of
many things and I don't say what I am thinking. That I
will stay. That when you return from healing Mistress
whether she is live or no I am here with you always.
Never never without you. Here I am not the one to

throw out. No one steals my warmth and shoes because I am small. No one handles my backside. No one whinnies like sheep or goat because I drop in fear and weakness. No one screams at the sight of me. No one watches my body for how it is unseemly. With you my body is pleasure is safe is belonging. I can never not have you have me.

I am calm when you leave although you do not touch me close. Or put your mouth to mine. You saddle up and ask me to water the bean shoots and collect the eggs. I go there but the hens make nothing so I know a minha mãe is coming soon. The boy Malaik is near. He sleeps behind the door to where you do. I am calm, quiet, knowing you are very soon here again. I take off Sir's boots and lie on your cot trying to catch the fire smell of you. Slices of starlight cut through the shutters. A minha mãe leans at the door holding her little boy's hand, my shoes in her pocket. As always she is trying to tell me something. I tell her to go and when she fades I hear a small creaking. In the dark I know he is there. Eyes big, wondering and cold. I rise and come to him and ask what. What Malaik, what. He is silent but the hate in his eyes is loud. He wants my leaving. This cannot happen. I feel the clutch inside. This expel can never happen again.

I dream a dream that dreams back at me. I am on my knees in soft grass with white clover breaking through. There is a sweet smell and I lean close to get it. But the perfume goes away. I notice I am at the edge of a lake. The blue of it is more than sky, more than any blue I know. More than Lina's beads or the heads of chicory. I am loving it so, I can't stop. I want to put my face deep there. I want to. What is making me hesitate, making me not get the beautiful blue of what I want? I make me go nearer, lean over, clutching the grass for balance. Grass that is glossy, long and wet. Right away I take fright when I see my face is not there. Where my face should be is nothing. I put a finger in and watch the water circle. I put my mouth close enough to drink or kiss but I am not even a shadow there. Where is it hiding? Why is it? Soon Daughter Jane is kneeling next to me. She too looks in the water. Oh, Precious, don't fret, she is saying, you will find it. Where I ask, where is my face, but she is no more beside me. When I wake a minha mãe is standing by your cot and this time her baby boy is Malaik. He is holding her hand. She is moving her lips at me but she is holding Malaik's hand in her own. I hide my head in your blanket.

I know you will come but morning does and you do not. All day. Malaik and me wait. He stays as far from me as he can. I am inside, sometimes in the garden but never in the lane where he is. I am making me quiet but I am loose inside not knowing how to be. Horses move in someone's pasture beyond. The colts are tippy-toe and never still. Never still. I watch until it is too black to see. No dream comes that night. Neither does a minha mãe. I lie where you sleep. Along with the sound of blowing wind there is the thump of my heart. It is louder than the wind. The fire smell of you is leaving the pallet. Where does it go I wonder. The wind dies down. My heartbeat joins the sound of mice feet.

In the morning the boy is not here but I prepare porridge for us two. Again he is standing in the lane hold-

ing tight the corn-husk doll and looking toward where
you ride away. Sudden looking at him I am remembering the dog's profile rising from Widow Ealing's kettle.
Then I cannot read its full meaning. Now I know how. I
am guarding. Otherwise I am missing all understanding
of how to protect myself. First I notice Sir's boots are
gone. I look all around, stepping through the cabin, the
forge, in cinder and in pain of my tender feet. Bits of
metal score and bite them. I look and see the curl of a
garden snake edging toward the threshold. I watch its
slow crawl until it is dead in the sunlight. I touch your
anvil. It is cool and scraped smooth but it sings the heat
it lives for. I never find Sir's boots. Carefully, on my toes
I go back into the cabin and wait.

The boy quits the lane. He comes in but will neither
eat nor talk. We stare at each other across the table. He
does not blink. Nor me. I know he steals Sir's boots that
belong to me. His fingers cling the doll. I think that
must be where his power is. I take it away and place it
on a shelf too high for him to reach. He screams
screams. Tears falling. On bleeding feet I run outside to
keep from hearing. He is not stopping. Is not. A cart
goes by. The couple in it glance but do not greet or
pause. Finally the boy is silent and I go back in. The doll
is not on the shelf. It is abandon in a corner like a precious child no person wants. Or no. Maybe the doll is
sitting there hiding. Hiding from me. Afraid. Which?
Which is the true reading? Porridge drips from the
table. The stool is on its side. Seeing me the boy returns
to screaming and that is when I clutch him. I am trying
to stop him not hurt him. That is why I pull his arm. To
make him stop. Stop it. And yes I do hear the shoulder

crack but the sound is small, no more than the crack a wing of roast grouse makes when you tear it, warm and tender, from its breast. He screams screams then faints. A little blood comes from his mouth hitting the table corner. Only a little. He drops into fainting just as I hear you shout. I don't hear your horse only your shout and know I am lost because your shout is not my name. Not me. Him. Malaik you shout. Malaik.

Seeing him still and limp on the floor with that trickle of red from his mouth your face breaks down. You knock me away shouting what are you doing? shouting where is your ruth? With such tenderness you lift him, the boy. When you see the angle of his arm you cry out. The boy opens his eyes then faints once more when you twist it back into its proper place. Yes, there is blood. A little. But you are not there when it comes, so how do you know I am the reason? Why do you knock me away without certainty of what is true? You see the boy down and believe bad about me without question. You are correct but why no question of it? I am first to get the knocking away. The back of your hand strikes my face. I fall and curl up on the floor. Tight. No question. You choose the boy. You call his name first. You take him to lie down with the doll and return to me your broken face, eyes without glee, rope pumps in your neck. I am lost. No word of sorrow for knocking me off my feet. No tender fingers to touch where you hurt me. I cower. I hold down the feathers lifting.

Your Mistress recovers you say. You say you will hire someone to take me to her. Away from you. Each word that follows cuts.

Why are you killing me I ask you.

I want you to go.

Let me explain.

No. Now.

Why? Why?

Because you are a slave.

What?

You heard me.

Sir makes me that.

I don't mean him.

Then who?

You.

What is your meaning? I am a slave because Sir trades for me.

No. You have become one.

How?

Your head is empty and your body is wild.

I am adoring you.

And a slave to that too.

You alone own me.

Own yourself, woman, and leave us be. You could have killed this child.

No. Wait. You put me in misery.

You are nothing but wilderness. No constraint. No mind.

You shout the word—mind, mind, mind—over and over and then you laugh, saying as I live and breathe, a slave by choice.

On my knees I reach for you. Crawl to you. You step back saying get away from me.

I have shock. Are you meaning I am nothing to you?

That I have no consequence in your world? My face absent in blue water you find only to crush it? Now I am living the dying inside. No. Not again. Not ever. Feathers lifting, I unfold. The claws scratch and scratch until the hammer is in my hand.

Jacob Vaark climbed out of his grave to visit his beautiful house.

"As well he should," said Willard.

"I sure would," answered Scully.

It was still the grandest house in the whole region and why not spend eternity there? When they first noticed the shadow, Scully, not sure it was truly Vaark, thought they should creep closer. Willard, on the other hand, knowledgeable about spirits, warned him of the consequences of disturbing the risen dead. Night after night they watched, until they convinced themselves that no one other than Jacob Vaark would spend haunting time there: it had no previous tenants and the Mistress forbade anyone to enter. Both men respected, if they did not understand, her reasoning.

For years the neighboring farm population made up

the closest either man would know of family. A good-hearted couple (parents), and three female servants (sisters, say) and them helpful sons. Each member dependent on them, none cruel, all kind. Especially the master who, unlike their more-or-less absent owner, never cursed or threatened them. He even gave them gifts of rum during Christmastide and once he and Willard shared a tipple straight from the bottle. His death had saddened them enough to disobey their owner's command to avoid the poxed place; they volunteered to dig the last, if not the final, grave his widow would need. In dousing rain they removed five feet of mud and hurried to get the body down before the hole filled with water. Now, thirteen days later, the dead man had left it, escaped his own grave. Very like the way he used to reappear following weeks of traveling. They did not see him—his definitive shape or face—but they did see his ghostly blaze. His glow began near midnight, floated for a while on the second story, disappeared, then moved ever so slowly from window to window. With Master Vaark content to roam his house and not appear anywhere else, scaring or rattling anybody, Willard felt it safe and appropriate for him and Scully to stay loyal and help the Mistress repair the farm; prepare it also, for nothing much had been tended to after she fell ill. June on its way and not a furrow plowed. The shillings she offered was the first money they had ever been paid, raising their work from duty to dedication, from pity to profit.

There was much to be done because, hardy as the women had always been, they seemed distracted, slower,

now. Before and after the blacksmith healed Mistress
and the girl, Florens, was back where she belonged, a
pall had descended. Still, Willard said, Lina continued
to do her work carefully, calmly, but Scully disagreed,
said she was simmering. Like green apples trembling in
boiling water too long, the skin near to breaking, needing quick removal, cooling before mashed into sauce.
And Scully should know since he had wasted hours over
the years secretly watching her river baths. Unfettered
glimpses of her buttocks, that waist, those syrup-colored
breasts, were no longer available. Mainly he missed what
he never saw elsewhere: uncovered female hair, aggressive, seductive, black as witchcraft. Seeing its wet cling
and sway on her back was a quiet joy. Now, no more.
Wherever, if ever, she bathed he was convinced she was
about to burst.

Mistress had changed as well. The mourning, said
Willard, the illness—the effects of all of that were plain
as daylight. Her hair, the brassy strands that once
refused her cap, had become pale strings drifting at her
temples, adding melancholy to her newly stern features.
Rising from her sickbed, she had taken control, in a
manner of speaking, but avoided as too tiring tasks she
used to undertake with gusto. She laundered nothing,
planted nothing, weeded never. She cooked and
mended. Otherwise her time was spent reading a Bible
or entertaining one or two people from the village.

"She'll marry again, I reckon," said Willard. "Soon."

"Why soon?"

"She's a woman. How else keep the farm?"

"Who to?"

Willard closed one eye. "The village will provide." He coughed up a laugh recalling the friendliness of the deacon.

Sorrow's change alone seemed to them an improvement; she was less addle-headed, more capable of handling chores. But her baby came first and she would postpone egg-gathering, delay milking, interrupt any field chore if she heard a whimper from the infant always somewhere nearby. Having helped with her delivery, they assumed godfather status, even offering to mind the baby if Sorrow needed them to. She declined, not because she did not trust them; she did, but out of a need to trust herself.

Strangest was Florens. The docile creature they knew had turned feral. When they saw her stomping down the road two days after the smithy had visited Mistress' sickbed and gone, they were slow to recognize her as a living person. First because she was so blood-spattered and bedraggled and, second, because she passed right by them. Surely a sudden burst of sweating men out of roadside trees would have startled a human, any human, especially a female. But this one neither glanced their way nor altered her pace. Both men, breathless and still spooked from a narrow escape, leaped out of her path. In their frightened minds anything could be anything. Both were running as fast as they could back to the livestock under their care before the hogs ate their litter. Much of the morning they had spent hiding from an insulted bear, a harrowing incident they agreed was primarily Willard's fault. The netted partridge hanging from the older man's waist was supplement enough for

two meals each. It was reckless to press their good fortune and linger just so he could rest beneath a beech and
puff his pipe. Both knew what a whiff of smoke could
do in woods where odor was decisive: to flee, attack,
hide or, as in the case of a sow bear, investigate. When
the laurel hell that had yielded the partridges suddenly
crackled, Willard stood up, holding his hand out to
Scully for silence. Scully touched his knife and stood
also. After a moment of uncanny quiet—no birdcalls or
squirrel chatter—the smell washed over them at the
same moment the sow crashed through the laurel click-
ing her teeth. Not knowing which of them she would
select, they separated, each running man hoping he had
made the correct choice, since play possum was not an
option. Willard ducked behind an outcropping, thumb
tamped his pipe and prayed the ledge of slate would dis-
able the wind's direction. Scully, certain he felt hot
breath on his nape, leaped for the lowest branch and
swung up onto it. Unwise. Herself a tree climber, the
bear had merely to stand up to clamp his foot in her
jaws. Scully's fear was not craven, however, so he determined to make at least one powerful gesture of defense
no matter how hopeless. He snatched out his knife,
turned and, without even aiming, rammed it at the head
of the agile black hulk below. For once desperation was
a gift. The blade hit, slid like a needle into the bear's eye.
The roar was terrible as, clawing bark, she tumbled to
the ground on her haunches. A ring of baying dogs
could not have enraged her more. Snarling, standing
straight up, she slapped at the stuck blade until it fell
out. Then down on all fours she rolled her shoulders

and wagged her head from side to side. It seemed to
Scully a very long time before the grunt of a cub got her
attention and, off balance by the blinding that dimin-
ished her naturally poor sight, she lumbered away to
locate her young. Scully and Willard waited, one treed
like a caught bear himself, the other hugging rock, both
afraid she would return. Convinced finally that she
would not, cautiously sniffing for the smell of fur, listening for a grunt, the movement of the other, or a return
of birdcall, they emerged. Slowly, slowly. Then raced. It
was when they shot from the wood onto the road that
they saw the female-looking shape marching toward
them. Later, when they discussed it, Scully decided she
looked less like a visitation than a wounded redcoat,
barefoot, bloody but proud.

Sold for seven years to a Virginia planter, young
Willard Bond expected to be freed at age twenty-one.
But three years were added onto his term for infrac-
tions—theft and assault—and he was re-leased to a
wheat farmer far up north. Following two harvests, the
wheat succumbed to blast and the owner turned his
property over to mixed livestock. Eventually, as over-
grazing demanded more and more pasture, the owner
made a land-for-toil trade with his neighbor, Jacob
Vaark. Still, one man could not handle all that stock.
The addition of a boy helped.

Before Scully's arrival, Willard had suffered hard and
lonesome days watching cattle munch and mate, his
only solace in remembering harder but more satisfying
days in Virginia. Brutal though that work was, the days
were not flat and he had company. There he was one of

twenty-three men working tobacco fields. Six English, one native, twelve from Africa by way of Barbados. No women anywhere. The camaraderie among them was sealed by their shared hatred of the overseer and the master's odious son. It was upon the latter that the assault was made. Theft of a shoat was invented and thrown in just to increase Willard's indebtedness. He had trouble getting used to the rougher, colder region he was moved into. At night in his hammock, trapped in wide, animated darkness, he braced himself against the living and the dead. The glittering eyes of an elk could easily be a demon, just as the howls of tortured souls might be the call of happy wolves. The dread of those solitary nights gripped his days. Swine, sheep and cattle were his sole companions, until the owner returned and carted away the best for slaughter. Scully's arrival was met with welcome and relief. And when their duties expanded to occasional help on the Vaark place, and they developed an easy relationship with its people, there were just a few times Willard overdrank and mis-behaved. Early on in his post, he had run away twice, only to be caught in a tavern yard and given a further extension of his term.

An even greater improvement in his social life began when Vaark decided to build a great house. Again, he was part of a crew of laborers, skilled and not, and when the blacksmith came, things got more and more inter-esting. Not only was the house grand and its enclosure impressive, its gate was spectacular. Sir wanted fancy work on both panels, but the smithy persuaded him no. The result was three-foot-high lines of vertical bars capped with a simple pyramid shape. Neatly these iron bars led to the gate each side of which was crowned by a flourish of thick vines. Or so he thought. Looking more closely he saw the gilded vines were actually serpents, scales and all, but ending not in fangs but flowers. When the gate was opened, each one separated its petals from the other. When closed, the blossoms merged.

He admired the smith and his craft. A view that lasted until the day he saw money pass from Vaark's hand to the blacksmith's. The clink of silver was as unmistakable as its gleam. He knew Vaark was getting rich from rum investments, but learning the blacksmith was being paid for his work, like the men who delivered building materials, unlike the men he worked with in Virginia, roiled Willard, and he, encouraging Scully, refused any request the black man made. Refused to chop chestnut, haul charcoal or work bellows and "forgot" to shield green lumber from rain. Vaark chastised them both into sullen accommodation, but it was the smithy himself who calmed Willard down. Willard had two shirts, one with a collar, the other more of a rag. On the morning he slipped in fresh dung and split the shirt all the way down its back, he changed into the good collared one. Arriving at the site, he caught the blacksmith's eye, then his nod, then his thumb pointing straight up as if to signal approval. Willard never knew whether he was being made fun of or complimented. But when the smithy said, "Mr. Bond. Good morning," it tickled him. Virginia bailiffs, constables, small children, preachers—none had ever considered calling him mister, nor did he expect them to. He knew his rank, but did not know the lift that small courtesy allowed him. Joke or not, that first time was not the last because the smithy never failed to address him so. Although he was still rankled by the status of a free African versus himself, there was nothing he could do about it. No law existed to defend indentured labor against them. Yet the smithy had charm and he did so enjoy being called mister. Chuckling to himself, Willard understood why the girl, Florens, was struck silly by the man. He probably called her miss or lady when they met in the wood for suppertime foolery. That would excite her, he thought, if she needed any more than just the black man's grin.

"In all my born days," he told Scully, "I never saw anything like it. He takes her when and where he wants and she hunts him like a she-wolf if he's not in her eye. If he's off at his bloomery for a day or two, she sulks till he comes back hauling the blooms of ore. Makes Sorrow look like a Quaker."

Only a few years older than Florens, Scully was less bewildered by the sharp change in her demeanor than Willard was. He thought of himself as an astute judge of character, felt he, unlike Willard, had a wily, sure-shot instinct for the true core of others. Willard judged people from their outside: Scully looked deeper. Although he relished Lina's nakedness, he saw a purity in her. Her loyalty, he believed, was not submission to Mistress or Florens; it was a sign of her own self-worth—a sort of keeping one's word. Honor, perhaps. And while he joined Willard in making fun of Sorrow, Scully preferred her over the other two servants. If he had been interested in seduction, that's who he would have chosen: the look of her was daunting, complicated, distant. The unblinking eyes, smoke gray, were not blank, but waiting. It was that lying-in-wait look that troubled Lina. Everyone but himself thought she was daft because she talked out loud when alone, but who didn't? Willard issued greetings to ewes regularly and Mistress always chatted directions to herself while at some solitary task. And Lina—she answered birds as if they were asking her advice on how to fly. To dismiss Sorrow as "the odd one" ignored her quick and knowing sense of her position. Her privacy protected her; her easy coupling a present to herself. When pregnant, she glowed and when her time came she sought help in exactly the right place from the right people.

On the other hand, if he had been interested in rape, Florens would have been his prey. It was easy to spot that combination of defenselessness, eagerness to please and, most of all, a willingness to blame herself for the meanness of others. Clearly, from the look of her now, that was no longer true. The instant he saw her marching down the road—whether ghost or soldier—he knew she had become untouchable. His assessment of her un-rape-ability, however, was impersonal. Other than a voyeur's obsession with Lina's body, Scully had no carnal interest in females. Long ago the world of men and only men had stamped him and from the first moment he saw him he never had any doubt what effect the black-smith would have on Florens. Thus her change from "have me always" to "don't touch me ever" seemed to him as predictable as it was marked.

Also Scully's opinion of Mistress was less generous

than Willard's. He did not dislike her but looked on her behavior after the master's death and her own recovery not simply as the effects of ill health and mourning. Mistress passed her days with the joy of a clock. She was a penitent, pure and simple. Which to him meant that underneath her piety was something cold if not cruel. Refusing to enter the grand house, the one in whose construction she had delighted, seemed to him a punishment not only of herself but of everyone, her dead husband in particular. What both husband and wife had enjoyed, even celebrated, she now despised as signs of both the third and seventh sins. However well she loved the man in life, his leaving her behind blasted her. How could she not look for some way to wreak a bit of vengeance, show him how bad she felt and how angry?

In his twenty-two years, Scully had witnessed far more human folly than Willard. By the time he was twelve he had been schooled, loved and betrayed by an Anglican curate. He had been leased to the Synod by his so-called father following his mother's death on the floor of the tavern she worked in. The barkeep claimed three years of Scully's labor to work off her indebtedness, but the "father" appeared, paid the balance due and sold his son's services, along with two casks of Spanish wine, to the Synod.

Scully never blamed the curate for betrayal nor for the flogging that followed, since the curate had to turn the circumstances of their being caught into the boy's lasciviousness, otherwise he would be not just defrocked but executed. Agreeing that Scully was too young to be permanently incorrigible, the elders passed him along to a landowner who needed a hand to work with a herdsman far away. A rural area, barely populated, where, they hoped, the boy might at best mend his ways or at worst have no opportunity to corrupt others. Scully anticipated running away as soon as he arrived in the region. But on the third day a violent winter storm froze and covered the land in three feet of snow. Cows died standing. Ice-coated starlings clung to branches drooping with snow. Willard and he slept in the barn among the sheep and cattle housed there, leaving the ones they could not rescue on their own. There in the warmth of animals, their own bodies clinging together, Scully altered his plans and Willard didn't mind at all. Although the older man liked drink, Scully, having slept beneath the bar of a tavern his whole childhood and seen its effects on his mother, avoided it. He decided to bide his time until, given the freedom fee, he was able to buy a horse. The carriage or cart or wagon drawn were not superior to the horse mounted. Anyone limited to walking everywhere never seemed to get anywhere.

As the years slid by he remained mentally feisty while practicing patience, even as his hopes were beginning to dim. Then Jacob Vaark died and his widow relied on himself and Willard so much, she paid them. In four months he had already accumulated sixteen shillings. Four pounds, maybe less, would secure a horse. And when the freedom fee—goods or crop or coin equaling twenty-five pounds (or was it ten?)—was added on, the years of peonage would have been worth it. He did not want to spend his life just searching for something to eat and love. Meanwhile he did nothing to disturb Mistress

Vaark or give her any cause to dismiss him. He was unnerved when Willard prophesied quick marriage for her. A new husband handling the farm could make very different arrangements, arrangements that did not include him. The opportunity to work for and among women gave both him and Willard advantage. However many females there were, however diligent, they did not fell sixty-foot trees, build pens, repair saddles, slaughter or butcher beef, shoe a horse or hunt. So while he watched the disaffection Mistress spread, he did all he could to please her. When she beat Sorrow, had Lina's hammock taken down, advertised the sale of Florens, he cringed inside but said nothing. Not only because it was not his place, but also because he was determined to be quit of servitude forever, and for that, money was a guarantee. Yet, when possible and in secret, he tried to soften or erase the hurt Mistress inflicted. He prepared a box for Sorrow's baby, lined it with sheepskin. He even tore down the advertisement posted in the village (but missed the one in the meetinghouse). Lina, however, was unapproachable, asking nothing and reluctant to accept whatever was offered. The hogshead cheese he and Willard had made was still wrapped in cloth in the toolshed where she now slept.

Such were the ravages of Vaark's death. And the consequences of women in thrall to men or pointedly without them. Or so he concluded. He had no proof of what was in their minds, but based on his own experience he was certain betrayal was the poison of the day.

Sad.

They once thought they were a kind of family

because together they had carved companionship out of isolation. But the family they imagined they had become was false. Whatever each one loved, sought or escaped, their futures were separate and anyone's guess. One thing was certain, courage alone would not be enough. Minus bloodlines, he saw nothing yet on the horizon to unite them. Nevertheless, remembering how the curate described what existed before Creation, Scully saw dark matter out there, thick, unknowable, aching to be made into a world.

Perhaps their wages were not as much as the blacksmith's, but for Scully and Mr. Bond it was enough to imagine a future.

I walk the night through. Alone. It is hard without Sir's boots. Wearing them I could cross a stony riverbed. Move quickly through forests and down hills of nettles. What I read or cipher is useless now. Heads of dogs, garden snakes, all that is pointless. But my way is clear after losing you who I am thinking always as my life and my security from harm, from any who look closely at me only to throw me away. From all those who believe they have claim and rule over me. I am nothing to you. You say I am wilderness. I am. Is that a tremble on your mouth, in your eye? Are you afraid? You should be. The hammer strikes air many times before it gets to you where it dies in weakness. You wrestle it from me and toss it away. Our clashing is long. I bare my teeth to bite you, to tear you open. Malaik is screaming. You pull my arms behind me. I twist away and escape you. The tongs are there, close by. Close by. I am swinging and swinging hard. Seeing you stagger and bleed I run. Then walk. Then float. An ice floe cut away from the riverbank in deep winter. I have no shoes. I have no kicking heart no home no tomorrow. I walk the day. I walk the night. The feathers close. For now.

It is three months since I run from you and I never before see leaves make this much blood and brass. Color so loud it hurts the eye and for relief I must stare at the heavens high above the tree line. At night when day-bright gives way to stars jeweling the cold black sky, I leave Lina sleeping and come to this room.

If you are live or ever you heal you will have to bend down to read my telling, crawl perhaps in a few places. I apologize for the discomfort. Sometimes the tip of the nail skates away and the forming of words is disorderly. Reverend Father never likes that. He raps our fingers and makes us do it over. In the beginning when I come to this room I am certain the telling will give me the tears I never have. I am wrong. Eyes dry, I stop telling only when the lamp burns down. Then I sleep among my words. The telling goes on without dream and when I wake it takes time to pull away, leave this room and do chores. Chores that are making no sense. We clean the chamber pot but are never to use it. We build tall crosses for the graves in the meadow then remove them, cut them shorter and put them back. We clean where Sir dies but cannot be anywhere else in this house. Spiders reign in comfort here and robins make nests in peace. All manner of small life enters the windows along with cutting wind. I shelter lamp flame with my body and bear the wind's cold teeth biting as though winter cannot wait to bury us. Mistress is not mindful of how cold the outhouses are nor is she remembering what night chill does to an infant. Mistress has cure but she is not well. Her heart is infidel. All smiles are gone. Each time she returns from the meetinghouse her eyes are nowhere and have no inside. Like the eyes of the women who examine me behind the closet door, Mistress' eyes only look out and what she is seeing is not to her liking. Her dress is dark and quiet. She prays much. She makes us all, Lina, Sorrow, Sorrow's daughter and me, no matter the weather, sleep either in the cowshed or the storeroom where bricks rope tools all manner of building waste are. Outside sleeping is for savages she says, so no more hammocks under trees for Lina and me even in fine weather. And no more fireplace for Sorrow and her baby girl because Mistress does not like the baby. One night of ice-cold rain Sorrow shelters herself and the baby here, downstairs behind the door in the room where Sir dies. Mistress slaps her face. Many times. She does not know I am here every night else she will whip me too as she believes her piety demands. Her churchgoing alters her but I don't believe they tell her to behave that way. These rules are her own and she is not the same. Scully and Willard say she is putting me up for sale. But not Lina. Sorrow she wants to give away but no one offers to take her. Sorrow is a mother. Nothing more nothing less. I like her devotion to her baby girl. She will not be called Sorrow. She has changed her name and is planning escape. She wants me to go with her but I have a thing to finish here. Worse is how Mistress is to

Lina. She requires her company on the way to church but sits her by the road in all weather because she cannot enter. Lina can no longer bathe in the river and must cultivate alone. I am never hearing how they once talk and laugh together while tending garden. Lina is wanting to tell me, remind me that she early warns me about you. But her reasons for the warning make the warning itself wrong. I am remembering what you tell me from long ago when Sir is not dead. You say you see slaves freer than free men. One is a lion in the skin of an ass. The other is an ass in the skin of a lion. That it is the withering inside that enslaves and opens the door for what is wild. I know my withering is born in the Widow's closet. I know the claws of the feathered thing did break out on you because I cannot stop them wanting to tear you open the way you tear me. Still, there is another thing. A lion who thinks his mane is all. A she-lion who does not. I learn this from Daughter Jane. Her bloody legs do not stop her. She risks. Risks all to save the slave you throw out.

There is no more room in this room. These words cover the floor. From now you will stand to hear me. The walls make trouble because lamplight is too small to see by. I am holding light in one hand and carving letters with the other. My arms ache but I have need to tell you this. I cannot tell it to anyone but you. I am near the door and at the closing now. What will I do with my nights when the telling stops? Dreaming will not come again. Sudden I am remembering. You won't read my telling. You read the world but not the letters of talk. You don't know how to. Maybe one day you will learn.

If so, come to this farm again, part the snakes in the gate you made, enter this big, awing house, climb the stairs and come inside this talking room in daylight. If you never read this, no one will. These careful words, closed up and wide open, will talk to themselves. Round and round, side to side, bottom to top, top to bottom all across the room. Or. Or perhaps no. Perhaps these words need the air that is out in the world. Need to fly up then fall, fall like ash over acres of primrose and mallow. Over a turquoise lake, beyond the eternal hemlocks, through clouds cut by rainbow and flavor the soil of the earth. Lina will help. She finds horror in this house and much as she needs to be Mistress' need I know she loves fire more.

See? You are correct. A minha mãe too. I am become wilderness but I am also Florens. In full. Unforgiven. Unforgiving. No ruth, my love. None. Hear me? Slave. Free. I last.

I will keep one sadness. That all this time I cannot know what my mother is telling me. Nor can she know what I am wanting to tell her. Mãe, you can have pleasure now because the soles of my feet are hard as cypress.

Neither one will want your brother. I know their tastes. Breasts provide the pleasure more than simpler things. Yours are rising too soon and are becoming irritated by the cloth covering your little girl chest. And they see and I see them see. No good follows even if I offered you to one of the boys in the quarter. Figo. You remember him. He was the gentle one with the horses and played with you in the yard. I saved the rinds for him and sweet bread to take to the others. Bess, his mother, knew my mind and did not disagree. She watched over her son like a hawk as I did over you. But it never does any lasting good, my love. There was no protection. None. Certainly not with your vice for shoes. It was as though you were hurrying up your breasts and hurrying also the lips of an old married couple.

Understand me. There was no protection and nothing in the catechism to tell them no. I tried to tell Reverend Father. I hoped if we could learn letters somehow someday you could make your way. Reverend Father was full of kindness and bravery and said it was what God wanted no matter if they fined him, imprisoned him or hunted him down with gunfire for it as they did other priests who taught we to read. He believed we would love God more if we knew the letters to read by. I don't know that. What I know is there is magic in learning.

When the tall man with yellow hair came to dine, I saw he hated the food and I saw things in his eyes that said he did not trust Senhor, Senhora or their sons. His way, I thought, is another way. His country far from here. There was no animal in his heart. He never looked at me the way Senhor does. He did not want.

I don't know who is your father. It was too dark to see any of them. They came at night and took we three including Bess to a curing shed. Shadows of men sat on barrels, then stood. They said they were told to break we in. There is no protection. To be female in this place is to be an open wound that cannot heal. Even if scars form, the festering is ever below.

Insults had been moving back and forth to and fro for many seasons between the king of we families and the king of others. I think men thrive on insults over cattle, women, water, crops. Everything heats up and finally the men of their families burn we houses and collect those they cannot kill or find for trade. Bound with vine one to another we are moved four times, each time more trading, more culling, more dying. We increase in number or we decrease in number until maybe seven times ten or ten times ten of we are driven into a holding pen. There we see men we believe are ill or dead. We soon learn they are neither. Their skin was confusing. The men guarding we and selling we are black. Two have hats and strange pieces of cloth at their throats. They assure we that the whitened men do not want to eat we. Still it is the continue of all misery. Sometimes we sang. Some of we fought. Mostly we slept or wept. Then the whitened men divided we and placed we in canoes. We come to a house made to float on the sea. Each water, river or sea, has sharks under. The whitened ones guarding we like that as much as the sharks are happy to have a plentiful feeding place.

I welcomed the circling sharks but they avoided me as if knowing I preferred their teeth to the chains around my neck my waist my ankles. When the canoe heeled, some of we jumped, others were pulled under and we did not see their blood swirl until we alive ones were retrieved and placed under guard. We are put into the house that floats on the sea and we saw for the first time rats and it was hard to figure out how to die. Some of we tried; some of we did. Refusing to eat the oiled yam. Strangling we throat. Offering we bodies to the sharks that follow all the way night and day. I know it was their pleasure to freshen us with a lash but I also saw it was their pleasure to lash their own. Unreason rules here. Who lives who dies? Who could tell in that moaning and bellowing in the dark, in the awfulness? It is one matter to live in your own waste; it is another to live in another's.

Barbados, I heard them say. After times and times of puzzle about why I could not die as others did. After pretending to be so in order to get thrown overboard. Whatever the mind plans, the body has other interests. So to Barbados where I found relief in the clean air and standing up straight under a sky the color of home. Grateful for the familiar heat of the sun instead of the steam of packed flesh. Grateful too for the earth supporting my feet never mind the pen I shared with so many. The pen that was smaller than the cargo hold we sailed in. One by one we were made to jump high, to bend over, to open our mouths. The children were best at this. Like grass trampled by elephants, they sprang up to try life again. They had stopped weeping long ago. Now, eyes wide, they tried to please, to show their ability and therefore their living worth. How unlikely their survival. How likely another herd will come to destroy them. A herd of men of heaped teeth fingering the hasps of whips. Men flushed red with cravings. Or, as I came to learn, destroyed by fatal ground life in the cane we were brought there to harvest. Snakes, tarantulas, lizards they called gators. I was burning sweat in cane only a short time when they took me away to sit on a platform in the sun. It was there I learned how I was not a person from my country, nor from my families. I was negrita. Everything. Language, dress, gods, dance, habits, decoration, song—all of it cooked together in the color of my skin. So it was as a black that I was purchased by Senhor, taken out of the cane and shipped north to his tobacco plants. A hope, then. But first the mating, the taking of me and Bess and one other to the curing shed.

Afterwards, the men who were told to break we in apologized. Later an overseer gave each of us an orange. And
it would have been all right. It would have been good
both times, because the results were you and your
brother. But then there was Senhor and his wife. I began
to tell Reverend Father but shame made my words nonsense. He did not understand or he did not believe. He
told me not to despair or be faint of heart but to love
God and Jesus Christ with all my soul; to pray for the
deliverance that would be mine at judgment; that no
matter what others may say, I was not a soulless animal,
a curse; that Protestants were in error, in sin, and if I
remained innocent in mind and deed I would be welcomed beyond the valley of this woeful life into an everlasting one, amen.

But you wanted the shoes of a loose woman, and
a cloth around your chest did no good. You caught
Senhor's eye. After the tall man dined and joined Senhor
on a walk through the quarters, I was singing at the
pump. A song about the green bird fighting then dying
when the monkey steals her eggs. I heard their voices
and gathered you and your brother to stand in their
eyes.

One chance, I thought. There is no protection but
there is difference. You stood there in those shoes and
the tall man laughed and said he would take me to
close the debt. I knew Senhor would not allow it. I said
you. Take you, my daughter. Because I saw the tall man
see you as a human child, not pieces of eight. I knelt
before him. Hoping for a miracle. He said yes.

It was not a miracle. Bestowed by God. It was a

mercy. Offered by a human. I stayed on my knees. In the dust where my heart will remain each night and every day until you understand what I know and long to tell you: to be given dominion over another is a hard thing; to wrest dominion over another is a wrong thing; to give dominion of yourself to another is a wicked thing.

Oh Florens. My love. Hear a tua mãe.

A NOTE ON THE TYPE

This book was set in Adobe Garamond. Designed for the Adobe Corporation by Robert Slimbach, the fonts are based on types first cut by Claude Garamond (c. 1480–1561). Garamond was a pupil of Geoffroy Tory and is believed to have followed the Venetian models, although he introduced a number of important differences, and it is to him that we owe the letter we now know as "old style." He gave to his letters a certain elegance and feeling of movement that won their creator an immediate reputation and the patronage of Francis I of France.

Designed by Virginia Tan
Map courtesy of the American Antiquarian Society